SHOOTING STAR

The Author would like to thank;

My awesome editor and friend:
James R. Woestman

My brilliant support tech and friend:
Robert J. Hornickel

Molly @ We Got You Covered Book Design for doing
an amazing job on my formatting and cover design.

My Caleb and Cammie for encouraging their mommy
to pursue her dream of being an author. Thank you for
making parenting so easy and such a joy. You are the
happiness in my life. I love you both so very much.

SKY WALKER
SHOOTING
STAR

Cynthia L. McDaniel

SHOOTING STAR

ISBN- 978-1-7325796-1-3

This book is luvingly dedicated to my Uncle Mike, Aunt Betty, and Aunt Annie. Thank you for being my second parents, my prayer partners, great advice givers and encouraging me on my crazy writing journey. I love you so much and thank God everyday for you.

"If you don't take risks, You'll have a wasted soul. "

- Drew Barrymore -

Chief Master Sergeant Bryant
Command Post 270***, Texas

November 25, 2019

Dear Sirs,

This letter serves as notification of the death of one female, Airman [NAME REDACTED] , [AGE REDACTED]. Due to the classified level of this mission, other identifiers are being withheld until further notice from command. As previously discussed, this casualty remains under investigation and as of today it has been confirmed accidental. Female died of blunt force trauma from failure of her government issued parachute.

Female, caucasian.
120 pounds
Hair: brown, eyes: blue.
Distinguishing marks: gray Saturn ring tattoo, left inner antebrachial
Body is being held at an undisclosed location. Family members have not yet been notified.

We will be contacting you with more information this week.

Regards,
CMS Bryant

LATE CITY FINAL

Saturday, October 5, 2019/Mostly sunny, 59/

AMERICA'S SUPERGIRL?

THE ASSOCIATED PRESS

The eyes of the country rest today on the tiny island of Oahu, Hawaii, after numerous amatuer videos have surfaced on social media of a young woman who appears to be flying. Witness accounts state first responders rushed to the airport after it was reported an aircraft in distress was headed toward the airfield. Instead of an aircraft, witnesses were astounded to see a woman descending freefall from the clouds carrying another female who appeared to be unconscious.

"I couldn't believe what I was seeing and I still can't believe what I saw," an anonymous witness stated. "We waited for a parachute to appear above her, but at the rate of speed and the direction she was flying it would have been impossible. She landed, dropped off the female, then ran from the scene, no parachute strings in sight. If I hadn't videoed it myself, I wouldn't have believed it."

The witness further stated that a black SUV seemingly appeared from nowhere, snatching the mysterious flying girl from the runway. Various personal social media accounts that first posted the video have been suspended, however the video has been shared millions of times and is still available to the public. Repeated requests for comment from the Air Force and officials at Hickam Air Force Base have been ignored or denied.

ONE

A LOUD SNAP of lightning woke me from my sleep. My eyes shot open, then closed again to adjust to the dim lit room. The familiar smell of salty, Hawaiian ocean air mixed with a soft scent of vanilla filled my senses. I slowly blinked open my eyes to a bombay palm ceiling fan spinning softly above me. Where was I? Shouldn't I be back in my hometown of Clarksville? This bedroom was not familiar at all. I blinked again. The airfield. First responders. Phones pointed up at me. Faces filled with disbelief, eyes filled with horror. The last memories I had, slowly began to drain back in my mind. I groaned inwardly at the complexity of what I had done. They knew now. The whole world knew now. I can fly.

I sat slowly up in bed and listened for noises. Anything that would let me know where I was. A pain in my side reminded me again of my injury from the water spout I had been sucked into a couple of weeks ago during flight research. I lifted up my shirt and found my side wrapped tight with fresh medical tape, but didn't remember anyone wrapping me. In the distance the sound of a jet on approach let me know I couldn't be far from my Air Force base, Hickam.

I slid off the bed as quietly as possible, my bare feet sinking into the plush carpet, a sure sign I was not in a medical facility, but someone's home. I tiptoed to the white panel door, then paused to listen, curious as to what and who might be on the other side. The rain on the roof pounded harder and thunder shook the sky, making it impossible to hear much of anything. The door handle squeaked softly as I turned it, peeking out into a hallway where a shiny oak floor extended to the right of the door. A little further down I could see family pictures decorating the wall. My hand shook as I pulled a strand of my long, dark curly hair out of my eyes, then looked down to see if what I was wearing was something I could fight in if need be. It was comforting to see my familiar soft gray and orange shorts and matching University of Tennessee tee shirt. I could definitely pull off some jiu jitsu moves in this, if need be.

The sound of footsteps echoed down the hall and I immediately jumped behind the door and flew to the ceiling, laying my body flat against it. The door was gently pushed open and a tall, dark figure walked into the room. I glanced down toward the bed that looked obviously empty, as the person walked over and moved the covers around.

"Claire?" his deep voice whispered. Whoever he was, he was a big guy, at least 6'5". He walked around the bed, his voice sounding a little more frantic while calling my name again. I could clearly see a gun strapped to his waist as I layed still against the ceiling in the darkness of the room.

"*Ok Claire, what are you gonna do?*" I thought to myself, biting my lip nervously and trying to control my frantic breathing.

"Claire?" he said, a little louder, as he walked to the tall window and double checked the lock on it. He then quickly strided to the door and was just reaching for the light switch when I made my move and pounced on him from behind.

I threw my right arm around his neck attempting to choke him out. Much to my embarrassment, in one clean swope I was flipped when he easily hip tossed me over his head. He knelt down to his left knee, using my right arm as a lasso and put me right on my back. The light flipped on and I looked up into the amused upside down face of Mr. Lucas, my bodyguard the Air Force had assigned to me during travel. My mind immediately went back to the airfield, where his strong arm had reached from the back seat of the SUV and scoped me off the runway, rescuing me from the media frenzy.

"What are you doing Claire?" he gasped, slightly annoyed.

"Oh hey Mr. Lucas," I cringed, relieved to see him.

"That was humiliating."

His large hand reached down and enveloped mine and lifted me effortlessly off the floor.

"Are you ok? Are your ribs ok?"

"Yeah, that hurt though," I gasped.

"Well, what did you expect? You may be a supergirl, but can't nobody touch this," he chuckled, his perfect white teeth gleaming from his dark skin. He still reminded me so much of Will Smith in *Men In Black*, except Mr. Lucas was a good 20 pounds heavier and much taller. And when I say heavier, I mean muscular.

This guy was a monster, but a kind and patient one who made me feel safe and secure and boy, at this moment I needed that. "Let's get you downstairs and have you looked at," he said.

I cautiously followed him down the hallway and to a round set of stairs that descended into a spacious foyer. At the bottom of the stairs, two colorful potted tropical trees stood majestically on either side of the glass French entry doors and gleamed off the freshly polished pine hardwood. I did a double take on the doors when I noticed each glass square covered in brown paper. That was weird.

Voices from the kitchen caught my attention and I immediately recognized Lt. General Gray's, the General of Hickam.

We walked into a large black and white kitchen, where my eyes were drawn to the center of the room. Gathered around a bar were the familiar faces of Lt. General

Gray and his wife Corrin, Major Wang (who had been handling my medical care here in Oahu) and beside him Captain Crew and his wife, Anna. Everyone stopped talking and all eyes went on me.

After an awkward moment, Anna Crew got up from the bar and walked over, wrapping me in her arms. "Oh Claire," she said, her voice shaking with emotion, "how can we ever begin to thank you?"

"Careful with her ribs there," Major Wang called from the bar.

I softly hugged her back, unsure of what to say, but managed a quiet, "You're welcome, Mrs. Crew."

She leaned in, looking me in the eyes and taking my face in her hands. "I don't care what anyone says. You did the right thing. You saved my Kirsten's life and I will owe you for the rest of mine."

I smiled at her, while the unconscious face of Kirsten flashed across my mind, jogging my memory and making my heart drop in my chest. "Kirsten...is she ok?" I asked.

"She's going to be fine," Major Wang called again from the bar. We walked over and I found a seat, exhaustion washing over me again. "It was a close one, but you got her to the medics just in time."

I smiled slightly, but I knew despite that good news, I was in a lot of trouble.

"Are you feeling ok?" Lt. General Gray asked, sitting directly across from me.

As if on cue, I yawned, nodding my head slowly. "I feel ok. I'm just so tired." I rubbed my eyes and looked around the room. "Where am I?"

Corrin Gray, who was sitting beside me, put her arm around the back of my chair. "You're at our home, sweetie. We live on Hickam on the back side of the base. Don't worry Claire, you're safe. The Air Force has put extra surveillance on our house while you're here."

"Surveillance?..." I began to ask.

"You've been asleep for three days now," Major Wang explained. "Lt. General brought you here, because it's not safe for you at the hospital."

I nodded at him, worried he was here because something was wrong physically with me. Major Wang was the head doctor at Tripler, Hickam's top notch medical facility. "So you're here because..." I started to ask.

"Just to keep an eye on you," Major Wang smiled. "You're in perfect health. Just very fatigued."

"*Perfect health,*" I thought to myself. "*Did that mean that my body was back to normal?*" There had been some discussion in the past about the possibility of a blood transfusion and that scared me, not because of death, but out of fear of returning to normalcy. My flying power had been a result of an accident I had with a failed WWII military experiment, when a mysterious pink fluid mixed with my blood. If I had a blood transfusion, I feared everything would return to normal and I didn't want normalcy. I didn't want to lose my flying superpower. Outside of meeting my Johnny, it was the best thing that had ever happened to me.

Major Wang must have read my mind because he

smiled slightly. "Also, your blood type remains the same. Nothing has changed there either."

I breathed an obvious sigh of relief and heard a slight snicker. An awkward moment of silence soon followed, as everyone stole curious glances my way. Everyone here except for Lt. General Gray (and maybe his wife Corrin) had no idea about my flying power until the Kirsten Crew incident. I noticed her dad Captain Crew, (who was also my boss and had never been a big fan of mine) sat quietly at the far end of the bar. Maybe he was still in shock about my flying power or maybe he was embarrassed about the way he had treated me. Either way, I could tell he was terribly uncomfortable as he drummed his fingers on the counter, staring off into space.

The doorbell chimed, thankfully taking the focus off me.

"I got that," Mr. Lucas said, heading toward the foyer.

"Oh, that's probably the pizza guy," Corrin said, grabbing her wallet and following after him.

"You must be starving Claire," said Anna, her eyes squinting with concern like my mom did when she was worried about me. I missed my mom like crazy. "I know for a fact, you've barely eaten in three days."

I shrugged and smiled politely. "Maybe a little." Actually, I hadn't even thought about food. My mind was too full. As I sat at the bar, different images began flashing through my mind. Slowly the last three days were coming back. Temperature checks, waking up for a few moments to take a drink or foggy trips to the restroom, Major Wang examining my Saturn ring tat or

Corrin constantly checking on me.

"Well, you should definitely eat something," Lt. General said. "You need to get your energy back."

"Yes sir," I said, looking over at him, suddenly aware this was the first time I had ever seen him in his civies, or all the other higher ups for that matter. He leaned back on his stool looking completely comfortable in his Adidas sweatshirt and jeans. Little slivers of gray hair peaked out from his buzzed, dark brown hair and faint smile lines etched across his still boyish face. I didn't dare argue with him because even though I wasn't hungry, Lt. General was still an intimidating man, no matter what he was wearing.

Mr. Lucas soon returned carrying 3 large pizza boxes and set them on the kitchen island. Lt. General got up to help Corrin get out plates and napkins and soon everyone with the exception of me, were gathered around the pizza helping themselves.

I turned and looked out at the rain pelting the tall glass window, where at the top I could see the branches of a palm tree swaying erratically in the wind. I closed my eyes and imagined myself flying through the sky, the rain washing over me, completely free from the stresses down here. Thunder shook the sky again, lighting up the palm branches and reminding me of my island.

Just a forty minute flight for me, south of Oahu, sat a little deserted island I had discovered one night while flying above the Pacific. It was the most beautiful place I had ever seen in my 19 short years. The north side of the island was a lush tropical forest, full of bright colored flowers and the sweetest smells, that led to a wall of rocky cliffs. On the west side, tucked into those cliffs, I had found my little cave that had protected me from the elements during my weekend getaways there. The rest of the island was wrapped in a pure white sandy beach that stretched all the way around. What I wouldn't do to be there right now, sleeping in my little cave, listening to the rain pound on the beach just below.

"Haley," Lt. General called me by my last name, snapping me out of my daydream. "Eat," he commanded softly.

I obediently walked over to the counter and took the smallest slice of cheese pizza I could find, then joined the others in the dining room.

The conversation began with football and how well the University of Hawaii was doing this year. I slowly ate my pizza and tried to listen, but couldn't focus. The elephant in the room was obviously being ignored and I wished they would get to the real topic of conversation. I wanted to know how much trouble I was in and what my punishment would be for disobeying orders. Still they talked about everything but. Mr. Lucas caught my attention as I finished my last bite of pizza. I noticed him walking around the house, eating pizza with one hand and checking and double checking the windows, making sure they were locked with the other. What was he being so paranoid about? At last the ladies picked up plates and excused themselves to the living room, a sure sign of what was finally coming.

Lt. General cleared his throat and took a sip of his water. "Ok Claire, just so you understand what is going on, I'm going to go over your schedule for the next few days."

"Schedule?" I asked. "But I already have a schedule."

Lt. General looked at me pointedly. "Claire, that schedule is over. Don't you understand? Your life will never be the same again. As of yesterday, your face is on the cover of every newspaper, magazine, and social media outlet all over the world. There's no more normalcy for you." His tone softened a little. "I'm not trying to scare you, but I'm trying to help you see the reality at hand. You will never know any kind of normal schedule or life again."

Lt. General nodded at Captain Crew, who then slid a newspaper article across the table to me. "*Oh no, not another article,*" I thought.

I looked down at the newspaper. *The New York Post* had a large picture of me descending from the sky carrying an unconscious Kirsten, covering half the front page. My face froze and I flushed a bright red, then broke out in my usual nervous hives. I began reading to myself while they waited patiently.

"*...witnesses were astounded to see a woman descending from the clouds...*"

"*...I couldn't believe what I was seeing...*"

"*...a black SUV seemed to appear from nowhere, snatching the mysterious flying girl from the runway...*"

"*...Repeated requests from the Air Force and Officials at Hickam Air Force base have been ignored...*"

I finished reading the article and slowly slid it back across the table, unsure of what to say. A dark cloud settled over my mind as I remembered the words of CMS Bryant, my commander at the secret government research compound the Air Force had sent me to, outside of Houston. I had been there just this past spring and we had discussed what would happen if the world found out about my flying superpower.

"*We have other countries spying on us at all times,*" he had told me. "*If they find out about you, we worry that you would become a target for them.*"

I had never given that much thought and had pretty much tucked it away without thinking that could ever be a possibility, until now.

"I'm...I'm sorry Lt. General," I finally managed. "I thought I was doing the right thing." I bit my bottom lip, trying to control my words to not avail. "I mean, I feel like I did the right thing...still."

I looked over at Captain Crew, who smiled ever so slightly at me. That was the first time I had ever seen anything even close to a smile from him and despite his harsh nature, I could tell he was genuinely grateful I had saved his daughter's life.

"Claire, we're not saying that what you did was morally wrong." Lt. General said. "On a personal level we are all so grateful for what you did for Kirsten and the Crews, but your disregard for the boundaries we have given you is a big problem. Just know that you have put us and the Air Force, well the American military for that matter, in a really bad spot."

I looked down at the table in shame. As an Airman that was the last thing you would ever want to hear. To bring any extra worries to your superiors or your country. I knew I had caused a lot of trouble. "I'm so sorry Lt. General. I tried to make what I thought was a good decision."

"Why didn't you come to me for help?" he asked. "I told you from the beginning, I'm here for you if you need anything."

"Besides that Claire, you could have killed yourself," Major Wang said. "We are still trying to figure out your body and the side effects of all this. We could barely keep you awake for the past three days..."

"...and what if you had fallen out of the sky with Kirsten?" Lt. General asked. "Mr. Lucas said you fainted within a minute of him getting you in the SUV."

I sat quietly, realizing I had no rebuttal for that. They were right as far as all that goes. I couldn't imagine going through all I did to save Kirsten, only to fall out of the sky and kill us both. Although I was a full two years into this whole ordeal, there were so many unanswered questions about my flying abilities. Obviously I had learned carrying someone for prolonged periods of time was not something my body could handle. I also knew that Major Kearney, the NASA scientist who had created this potion that gave me the power to fly, had mysteriously fallen out of the sky and died.

But still, I had few regrets. Kirsten was only 17 and

(excuse my brashness) instead of floating at the bottom of the Pacific right now, she was home and safe and out of the hands of the drug runners who had kidnapped her. How was that accomplished you may ask? Me. Little ol' me. I had risked my life to save her, using my flying power, newly acquired jiu jitsu skills, and a lot of luck.

A loud clap of thunder snapped me out of my thoughts. Lt. General and the guys were discussing my schedule for tomorrow between themselves. My eyes blinked in heaviness and I looked at the clock. It was 8:15 and it already felt like midnight.

"Ok Haley," Lt. General said. "Tomorrow at 08:00 Lucas will escort you to Tripler where Major Wang will do a full physical on you. At 10:00, you will be meeting with me and the same military officials you met with at Campbell and then your day will go from there. Understood?"

My eyes grew wide at the thought of that. The last time I had met with those guys, it was to send me here to Hickam, to hide me away from the rumors surrounding my flying power at home. Home for me by the way, was Ft. Campbell and Clarksville, Tennessee. I was almost positive it would be more of the same, only this time I would be permanently sent to the Houston compound. The thought of that was too much for me.

"Yes Sir," I said quietly, but I had so many questions. "Excuse me Sir, but do you think I'll be leaving Hickam?"

(I know I probably shouldn't haven't asked, but you have to understand, I am the most impatient person you'll ever meet. Twelve hours may not seem like a long time for some to wait, but for me it was like an eternity.)

Lt. General's eyes softened from the firm stare he had on me most of the night. "I'm not sure Claire. We'll be meeting in the morning while you're at the physical to discuss everything. Whatever we decide, it will be in the best interest of you. I can promise you that."

I sighed inwardly, knowing that answer was my ticket to a sleepless night. The next twelve hours were going to be torturous, with my mind full and my future hanging in the balance.

TWO

THAT NIGHT I laid in bed extremely tired, but more than that, curious about what Lt. General had said about me being all over social media. I pulled out my phone to do some internet surfing. I went to Youtube and typed in Oahu news and immediately the footage of me flying popped up. I watched wide eyed as someone, obviously one of the first responders, pointed their cell phone to the sky and narrated, awaiting what they thought was an aircraft in distress.

"Ok, so we're waiting here on the tarmac at the airfield for a plane that is supposed to be landing soon," a deep voice said into the camera. *"We received a plane in distress call from the Coast Guard, so yeah we're just waiting..."*

The area was quiet for a moment with the camera still scanning the sky, going back and forth up and down the shore line, while several voices could be heard talking about the surf.

"*What is that?*" I heard a female voice ask beside him.

"*Where? What are you talking about?*" he replied.

"*There! Can't you see it?*"

The camera pointed to the arm of the first responder lady and followed it up and into the blue clouds.

I sat up in bed, catching my breath, waiting for what I knew would be on the camera next. The guy searched the fuzzy cloud line, finally coming to a stop. A dark blurry speck came out of the bottom of one of the clouds. The camera adjusted and soon I came into focus, slowly descending, cradling Kirsten in my arms. I have to admit, it was a very creepy sight, as I almost appeared alien-like. I could immediately feel the sting in my muscles and the unbearable pain in my ribs return as I continued to watch. Today was Thursday. It had only been four days ago and it was all over the media.

"Is that?.." the guy started to ask.

"There's no way..." the lady responded, her voice shaking.

"How in the world?" he asked again.

Around him I could hear a rise in voices. Panic, lots of movement, shouting, OMGs and car doors slamming. This guy obviously, was not afraid and walked closer to where I was about to land.

Flashes of what I was seeing as I descended came back to me. I could see the astonishment in their faces and hear the fear in their voices. I did my best to hide my face behind Kirsten, but that wasn't much help.

Finally I landed and the guy came even closer, not saying a word, I just heard the heaviness of his breath and the wind blowing off the ocean and into his phone mic. Next the camera showed my best buddy Zhao running to me. He grabbed Kirsten as I untangled myself from the bungee cords I had used to strap her to me. His camera focused directly onto my terrified face, every feature of it in plain sight.

I saw Zhao look at me and heard him say it again. "Run Claire."

The camera then zoomed in on Zhao who turned and ran toward the first responders, yelling for help. A few brave souls went over to him and began administering aid to Kirsten. The camera panned back in search of me. By this time I was already running down the runway, a black SUV soon following in pursuit of me. I watched wide eyed as Mr. Lucas stepped out on the running board of the SUV and scooped me off the runway and in one millisecond we were gone.

I leaned back against my pillow. It was so surreal to watch it all unfold. No wonder why everyone was going crazy over this. The whole thing looked like a scene out of a Marvel movie, except it was obvious this was the real thing.

The next hour I researched everything I could on myself. The list on google was overwhelming. Every social media outlet, newspaper article, and magazine had plastered it everywhere the last four days. Previous videos taken of me over the last two years were popping up all over Youtube and Tiktok. They included me flying over the old buildings back home in my Halloween witch costume, the time I was caught flying over the fence to sneak in and meet Aerosmith after their concert, and finally me rescuing the girl from the accident at the bridge back home. Someone in Clarksville had given me the hashtag *Sky Walker* and now people were dumping all the information they could find on me there. They were beginning to tie everything in my past flying excursions to this one in Hawaii, so I could definitely see why Lt. General was so upset with me. My face was out there and there was no mistake about what I looked like. I shivered under my blanket. Now began their quest to find out who I was.

At 8 am sharp, I walked through a private back door and into Tripler Medical Center, in the shadow of a watchful Mr. Lucas. My Air Force uniform helped me blend more easily with the airmen here, but even so I kept my head down and shades on. My long curly hair was pulled back in a tight bun and tucked in at the base of my beret to further conceal my identity. I still felt like I stuck out like a sore thumb today though, and not because all eyes were on me. All eyes were on Mr. Lucas. In his black suit and dark shades, he was the one who looked like a character from an action movie, larger than life and oozing confidence and swag. I think it would have been more inconspicuous if I just came alone, but Lt. General Gray was adamant about me staying with Mr. Lucas. This whole kidnapping scenario had everyone on edge.

Major Wang greeted us as we got off the elevator and onto the fifth floor. A floor I was very familiar with. I usually came here every week for a short check in and check up, but I knew today would be much different.

"Ahhh Claire," Major Wang greeted me. "Come this way."

"I'll be here Claire," Mr. Lucas said pointing in the direction of a waiting room just down the hall.

I nodded and followed Major Wang a few doors down to a midsize room I had never been in before. He motioned for me to sit on the examining table, while a new nurse I had never seen before entered quickly behind him.

"Ok Charity," he instructed her. "Just her vitals and then you can go."

Charity glanced at me curiously and then proceeded to take all my vitals, double checking my blood pressure twice. She looked at my chart a little bewildered, then walked over to point out her findings to Major Wang, who then patted her on the shoulder and dismissed her with an "I see."

Charity shot an almost agitated glance at me and I quickly broke away from her stare and looked at the floor.

"Is everything ok?" I asked after she left, shutting the door behind her with a loud thud.

"Yes, just your heart rate is a little rapid for your age...

but not your condition."

"What do you mean?"

"You've never come in here without a rapid heart rate," he explained, looking at me over his glasses. "I never understood it...well, until now."

"Oh...well why do you think that is?" I pressed further.

"More than likely, it's because of the abnormalities in your blood, Claire. In all reality, you shouldn't even be alive. When I first drew your blood, I couldn't wrap my mind around what I was seeing, but I was given orders not to ask questions, so I didn't. I have so many though," he sighed as he pulled a needle out to draw my blood.

"I feel you, Major Wang," I agreed. "I'm two years into this with no explanation or answers."

"I wish I were Dr. York and was able to study what's happening with you. What gives your body the ability to defy gravity? It's so mind boggling." He found his favorite vein and quickly inserted the needle. I barely flinched. I was so used to it now.

I stared down at my tat on my wrist, twisting it in the sunlight, trying to make the pink color on it pop more. Major Wang filled two small vials of my pink tinted blood and then held one of them up in the sunlight. "Have you ever noticed how it shimmers in the sun?" he asked. "Almost like it has some kind of a metallic substance to it."

Hearing the words metallic immediately took me back to the Air Force hangar the night of the accident. I could still feel myself crashing down on the crate, hearing the sound of shattering glass, followed by a stinging pain in my wrist. And the smell. That weird metallic smell. How coincidental of Major Wang to bring that word up.

"You know Major Wang, the night of my accident, I could smell something metallic."

"What do you mean, Claire?" he asked. "Can you tell me how it happened?"

"Well, I was at the Air Force hangar visiting my boyfriend Johnny, who was pulling guard..."

"Your boyfriend is in the Air Force?" he interrupted.

"Army. He's a pilot. He flys Chinooks."

"Ahh, I see. Please go on."

"Well, he had me hide in this closet when Major Silva, his commanding officer, showed up unexpectedly. I thought the crate was safe to sit on, but when I did, it crashed to pieces. Inside were several glass tubes of this strange pink fluid and they sliced my wrist. The fluid mixed with my blood and the next thing I knew, I could fly."

"Fascinating," he said, then lightly grabbed my left wrist. "And the tattoo?"

"The tat was there the next day in place of my cut."

Major Wang examined it more closely. "It looks like there are some pink lines in it. From the potion?"

"I think so," I shrugged. "They get really bright when I'm flying...or even when I'm fixin' to fly."

"Fixing, huh?" he laughed, not taking his eyes off my wrist.

I smiled, blushing at my southern habit. "Yeah, fixin'."

"This is so incredible," he said, rubbing his fingers over

my tat. "It's almost like a superman/kryptonite scenario."

I tilted my head sideways, thoughtfully. "I never thought of it like that...but I guess I would rather be Supergirl than an alien."

Major Wang laughed, extending his hand to help me off the table. "Well Claire, excuse me...Supergirl, it looks like everything is still the same for you physically. I'm going to get this blood sample sent off to Dr. York in Houston and I'm sure if anything has changed with it, he'll let us know."

"Ok, thank you Major Wang," I said, hopping off the table.

Major Wang walked me down the hall to the waiting room. "Oh Claire, for the rest of the week, anytime you have a break, I want you to rest. Nothing other than orders on your schedule and nap whenever you get a chance, ok?"

"Yes Sir," I said, yawning on cue. That was definitely an order I would have no issue following.

I followed Mr. Lucas down the hall, passing Charity and a group of her nurse friends huddled at the nurses station and talking quietly amongst themselves. They all paused as we walked past, some staring knowingly at me and some glaring awkwardly at the floor.

"Put your shades on Claire," Mr. Lucas instructed me.

I slid them on, smiling slyly at the group. "Come on,

Mr. Lucas," I said loudly as we approached the elevator. "We better *fly* or we're going to be late." I emphasized the "fly" way too loud and way too long.

The elevator door dinged open and Mr. Lucas and I walked inside. "You gotta be smarty pants about all this?" he asked after the door closed.

"Well, they were all staring," I argued.

Mr. Lucas shook his head, rolling his eyes, his signature toothpick clenched between his teeth. "Well you better get used to it baby girl," he smiled. "Cause you got a lot of that coming."

THREE

MR. LUCAS AND I exited the same door we had entered and immediately jumped into an SUV that was waiting, doors open. Once inside, his phone rang.

"Yes Sir, all done here," he said after a moment. "Ok, I got it. Will do."

He hung up and looked up at the driver. "Sir, change of plans. 180th Special Forces Unit, please."

"My barracks?" I asked him. "Why are we going there?"

"We need to grab your personals. Remember? Gray said you're not staying there anymore."

"Yeah, but I didn't know it was permanent. I thought it was for just a few days until everything cooled down."

Mr. Lucas shrugged. "I don't know, Claire. Not my call. Take it up with the big man."

I sat back in my seat in frustration. I didn't want to

leave my barracks room. It had become home to me. I didn't want to leave my company. I had become so close with the guys I worked with, especially my buddy Zhao.

"I don't understand, Mr. Lucas. I mean, I get it...I disobeyed orders, but no one's paying attention to all the good I did."

Mr. Lucas, ever the calm one, looked over at me and lightly shrugged his shoulders. "If there's one thing I've learned, it's to always, always obey orders. There's a chain of command for a reason, Claire." I stared down at the ground and sighed because I knew there was truth to that. "...but," he continued, "for what it's worth, in *this* situation...I think you did the right thing." He lowered his voice. "That's just between you and I."

I smiled slightly at him, as we pulled up in front of my barracks. If Mr. Lucas agreed with me, I knew I did the right thing. I knew he had to make life and death decisions all the time.

"Well, Lt. General says keep the conversation light, because these guys know for sure what's up, Claire. We have an hour."

I nodded, knowing it wouldn't take me an hour. I came with very little because I had to leave Ft. Campbell so quickly, just 4 short months ago. As far as clothes go, all I had was two suitcases worth of what I had managed to grab on my weekend shopping trips to Walmart. It's weird how when you're in the military, clothes become a second priority. I spent most of my time in my BDU's, PT clothes, or something at least stamped with the Air

Force logo on it. I loved serving my country and I wore it proudly.

"You ready?" Mr. Lucas asked.

I took a deep breath. "Yes," I gulped and reached for the door handle.

"No ma'am, my side," he instructed me. He stepped out of the SUV and took a hard look around before opening the door the rest of the way. "Ok, let's go."

I followed close behind Mr. Lucas and up the sidewalk toward the two metal doors I had become so accustomed to entering. But this day it felt like a whole different building, a foreign place, and it seemed like I had been gone for months, even though it had only been a week.

Several of my air mates were standing around outside enjoying this beautiful September morning and as expected, all came to a standstill when I walked up.

I glanced at them, waving slightly as I moved quicker to keep pace with Mr. Lucas. He then opened the door, peeked inside the building, and motioned me inside.

"Let's go to your room," Mr. Lucas instructed me as once again, everyone in the foyer stopped to stare us down.

"Hey Haley," a few of them mumbled. I nodded and smiled back as genuinely as I could, but I recognized the feelings of betrayal in their stares. How could I have kept such a big secret from my teammates?

"It's on the fourth floor," I answered, "but Mr. Lucas,

I would like to stop and see Sgt. Mancuso. I feel like it's the right thing to do..to say goodbye."

Mr. Lucas nodded and followed me into the first office to the left, off the foyer. Sgt. Mancuso sat at his desk, staringing down at some paperwork. He looked up and his eyes popped open in surprise.

"Haley!" he gasped, then slowly got up and walked around his desk to greet me. "Are you ok?" he asked, putting both of his hands on my shoulders and looking me up and down, almost as if he was touching me to see if I was real.

"I'm fine, thank you Sgt. Mancuso. Is everything ok here?" I asked almost apologetically.

"We're all fine. Just..just a little astonished..as is everyone," he laughed nervously. "I still can't wrap my mind around it all...I don't even know what to say. I have so many questions."

"I know...and I'm so sorry. I would have told you if I could. The whole story. Maybe someday I can."

He smiled down at me. "No apologies needed. I'm just glad you're ok."

"Thank you Sergeant. Well, I came to grab my stuff." I pointed behind me. "I don't think I'll be back here, so I just wanted to say thank you for your patience and all you have taught me."

He smiled in appreciation. "You're welcome Airman Haley. You know if we could protect you properly, I would be fighting to keep you. Whether you realize it or not, you're a great asset to this company."

My eyes grew misty at his compliment. I had worked so hard to fit in and now that I did, I had to leave it all behind. I nodded my head in thanks, unable to say anything without losing it like a baby. I reached out to shake his hand and he grasped both his hands around mine.

"You stay safe Airman Haley," he smiled softly. "And that's an order."

"Yes Sir," I smiled.

Thirty minutes later, Mr. Lucas and I pretty much had my room packed and cleaned up. I stood in the echoing emptiness of my apartment, sadness and gloom surrounding me. Mr. Lucas must have noticed my depressive mood because he interrupted my thoughts with, "Would you like a moment alone?"

"Yes please," I answered.

He grabbed a few of my bags and waited outside the door. I walked over to my small balcony and slid the door open for the last time. The smell of salty ocean water filled my senses and took me back to my first day here. I was so lonely and homesick, but had quickly grown to love Hawaii. I closed my eyes and remembered all the warm nights I had spent flying off the balcony and into the night, over the vast Pacific Ocean. I had given up so much for the life of Kirsten Crew. I hope she was at least grateful.

I slid the door closed and grabbed my rolled up

bedding, then met Mr. Lucas in the hallway.

"We gotta move to make that meeting," he said. "You ready?"

"I guess," I sighed, shutting my door and not looking back. I knew what was to come. Another move, another room. I did not want to go.

FOUR

OUR SUV CAME to a stop in front of Hickam Headquarters. I followed Mr. Lucas up the steps to the building. The sun shined bright in the clear blue sky, a vast contrast to the heavy thunderstorm from last night. The only telltale signs were a few scattered palm tree leaves laying around the lawn.

I kind of felt sorry for Mr. Lucas. This guy was not only a part of the Secret Service, but obviously one of the best since they would fly him here in a private jet at the drop of a hat. Yet, here he was escorting me around an Air Force base. I'm sure he would much rather have been off on some cool secret mission somewhere, rescuing someone important.

"Claire!" I heard a familiar voice yell behind me.

I turned around to see my best buddy here on the

island, running up behind me.

"Zhao!" I squeaked in excitement.

Zhao picked me up in a bear hug, swinging me around and almost knocking his thick rimmed glasses off his face. I was so glad to see him. I hadn't seen him since we were on the runway and he was yelling at me to run.

"Omg Claire! I've been so worried about you! Where have you been? I've been asking and no one knows anything!" he gushed all at once.

I glanced at Mr. Lucas who shot me a warning look, so I quickly remembered not to share my whereabouts the past few days. "I've been around," I smiled. "They just kept me near Major Wang to make sure I'm physically ok."

Zhao squeezed me again. "Good, cause I was so worried!"

"What are you even doing here?" I asked.

"I'm here for the meeting. Me, my dad...I even saw Professor Corral."

"Professor Corral?" I asked, stunned that my jiu jitsu instructor was here. Thanks to him I learned my hands on techniques that I used to fight my way off the yacht Kirsten had been kidnapped on. "Have you talked to him?"

"No, I just saw him walk in with Lt. General...umm, he looked pretty shocked."

"Oh," I sighed, feeling guilty that someone else I was so close to, had to find out accidentally.

Mr. Lucas cleared his throat, nodding toward the door. Zhao looked him up and down, clearly impressed with my bodyguard.

"What are you doing hanging out with The Rock?" he asked under his breath, as we followed Mr. Lucas inside.

"Zhao!" I laughed, jabbing him in the arm.

Mr. Lucas led us upstairs to a hallway, where several men in their military suits stood guard in front of an open set of double doors.

"Are you nervous at all?" Zhao asked as we slowly approached the room.

"Nope," I said confidently, trying to make him believe me, even though I was scared to death.

"Yeah...ok," he laughed, as we walked into a conference room. This time there was no big fancy table like normal, instead a lone modest podium sat on a small stage in front of about 20 chairs. It almost reminded me of an old school press conference room, like the kind you would see in an early eighties TV crime series. It smelled of old wood, aged by the salty ocean air and didn't look like it had been used in awhile.

I scanned the room where familiar faces were all around me. Zhao's dad, Dr. Zhao (a small Asian man with glasses who was a mirror image of Zhao) sat with Command Sergeant Major Williams on the front row. I assumed they both would be here. Dr. Zhao was a scientist with NASA and his brilliance had been passed on to his son, which is why the Air Force had brought the younger Zhao to the island and teamed him up with me.

CSM Williams, another tall intimidating black man, had been at the meeting at Ft. Campbell and made the decision to send me here. I didn't know his exact job description, but it was definitely secretive, as he had come directly from Washington. I dreaded a face-to-face with him again, because he had made it clear to me before that no one had better find out about my flying power.

Lt. General Gray and Corrin, Major Wang, Captain and Anna Crew and Professor Corral all sat together on the front row talking in almost a whisper.

I nodded Zhao to the end of the second row of chairs and I sat as close as possible to the wall trying my best to stay inconspicuous.

"What do you think is going to happen?" Zhao whispered a moment after we sat down. "Do you think they'll send you back to Campbell?"

I sighed, "I'm not sure Zhao. They sent me here because things were too hot for me at Campbell. I don't know where else I would go."

Zhao looked at me sympathetically. "I don't want you to go Claire."

I was about to answer him, when out of the corner of my eye I saw Prof. Corral walk towards us. He sat down beside Zhao and leaned in close.

"Are you guys ok?"

Zhao leaned back slightly and they both looked at me.

"I'm fine, Professor B. I'm...I'm so sorry. I wish you didn't have to find out this way."

He smiled slightly, "It's ok, Claire..."

"No really," I interrupted him. "I asked so many times to tell you, but they wouldn't allow it."

He reached over and placed his hand on my arm.

"Claire, I'm sure they are doing what they believe is best for you. This is just all so unreal and unknown, so keeping you safe is what they are focused on."

I couldn't believe how calm Professor Corral was. Out of everyone, his reaction was definitely the coolest I had ever seen. Almost like he had been through this before.

Lt. General Gray tapped on the podium and cleared his throat, drawing our attention. Professor Corral squeezed my arm and quickly returned to his seat.

"Ok, if everyone could come in and find your seats."

I looked around to see who he was talking about. Wasn't this everybody? A few heads turned and I followed their gaze to the door where two more men and a young woman entered and sat in the back. I looked them over curiously. The female in particular caught my eye. She was small in stature just like me and couldn't have been no more than 25 years old. She had long brown hair tucked into a crisp bun and big brown eyes. She seemed extra timid as she followed the two men in. They were all dressed in a black uniform and beret with some pink insignia I had never seen before. I noticed they had also caught Zhao's eye and he glanced at me. I didn't even have to ask him who they were, because his eyes told me he had no idea either.

"Alright," Lt. General continued. "You are all here today, because we have an obvious breach of security. Each of you are going to be team players in keeping Claire safe and invisible from the public eye as much as we possibly can while she's at Hickam."

My heart fluttered. *Did that mean they were keeping me here?* Zhao looked at me out of the corner of his wide eye and I could see a glimmer of hope cross them.

"So, with that being said, we have some major decisions to make on behalf of Claire. We need to decide above all, what is best for her and where she belongs. As of 8 am this morning, Claire's identity is still widely unknown, but we know that it's just a matter of time now until that changes."

The room got eerily still. I swallowed hard and broke out into my usual nervous red blotchies, as several heads turned my way.

Lt. General continued, "We have been in talks with CSM Williams and other officials in charge of Claire's case and going back to the barracks is not going to be a possibility for her. There's just too much of a risk for her safety."

Why did he keep talking about me like I wasn't even here? I kept waiting for him to look my way and acknowledge me, but he kept talking to everyone but me.

"We've decided the safest place for her to be while she's here is in my home on Hickam with my wife Corrin, under heavy security. In three weeks, she will be flown to an undisclosed location until further notice."

I stared down at the floor, sure of where this undisclosed location was. I would be returning to the compound outside of Houston. That's where my doctor was and all the scientists that were studying my superpower. I didn't want to return there. It was ok once every quarter for my week-long check up, but there was no way I could live there. Being away from my family and Johnny was difficult in Hawaii, but it would be unbearable in the middle of nowhere in Texas. It was clear to me I was being punished. Punished for my disobedience.

"What? Seriously?" I heard Zhao whisper under his breath.

"So in the meantime, we are all going to do our best to keep Claire safe. She will still be completing her duties as an Airman, but in a different capacity." He turned to Prof. Corral. "Braulio, we want to keep up her sessions with you. Self defense is something we want Claire to become more practiced in, but as far as being in the population with other Airmen, that won't be happening." He turned to CSM Williams. "CSM Williams?"

CSM Williams walked to the podium. "I just want to remind each of you that you are here because you have knowledge of who Claire is. It has been our desire to see her identity kept secret.." he sighed heavily and did a side glance my way, "but since this is where we are, we are asking for your help in keeping her identity concealed. Like Lt. General stated, it's not a matter of if her identity will be revealed, but a matter of when. We've been asked to keep her here until things can calm down." CSM Williams walked around the podium and lowered his voice. "Right now there's just too many eyes and too many news crews on the island. Our fear is that flights to and from the island are being watched by both domestic and foreign eyes and we want her to lay low until the heat is off.

Any questions before we move on?" He looked around the room, then returned behind the podium, obviously ready to start another subject.

I continued staring at the floor. He didn't bother to glance my way when he asked if anyone had any questions. Come to think of it, no one had bothered to ask my opinion up to this point, ever. From the time I was first interrogated by Major Silva at Ft. Campbell, to my meetings at the compound in Houston and then here, no one had ever asked how I felt about any of this. No one asked where I wanted to live or what I thought should happen...and this was *my* life. Instead, decisions were made for me and I had obediently followed through.

I don't know if it was the stress of the past week or the lack of sleep finally catching up with me, but images of my mom, Johnny, and Kass flashed across my eyes and I slowly stood to my feet. Heads turned in my direction and CMS Williams finally looked up and noticed.

"Airman Haley?" he asked.

I felt all eyes on me; Zhao's directly below me, Mr. Lucas' steady glance from the back, and the inquisitive stare of the two guys and girl in the mysterious black uniforms. I cleared my throat and felt my neck and cheeks grow hot.

"Yes Sir," I said, my normally quiet voice stronger than what I thought it would be. "I'm just wondering if anyone has thought to consider my feelings in all of this. With all due respect, no one has ever asked. Instead I'm...I'm just moved from one place to the next. I mean, is there an end plan in all of this for me or do I spend the rest of my life hopping between air bases and hiding out?"

I took a deep breath and the room grew quiet again. CSM Williams looked wide eyed at me, obviously caught off guard by my questioning. I could tell I agitated him, as his glare bore deep into my confidence that was now shrinking significantly with each passing second. He made it obvious to everyone he was carefully choosing his words before he spoke back to me. The whole room waited in thick anticipation for his reply.

"Airman Haley," he said at last, "It was made very clear to you in our first discussion at Campbell what you were to do at Hickam. You broke the rules that were given to you, while we trusted you to come here and do what we asked. Nothing more. Now, because of this, Hickam is on lockdown and our military is left to clean up after the hysteria this has created." He then walked slowly to my side of the room, his arms folded, staring me down. Out of the corner of my eye, I could see Zhao squirm nervously in his chair. CSM Williams was definitely an intimidating man. "Are you familiar with the term Court Martial, Airman Haley? Because let me tell you, that idea has surfaced in light of what has happened here."

I lowered my head, embarrassed by the principal/ student scolding I was receiving. I blinked hard, trying to catch my breath, at the mention of a possible court martialing. More than anything I wanted to be a good Airman, do my part to protect my country, and not add stress to it or anyone. For a moment I felt ashamed and embarrassed, but then Kirsten's unconscious face appeared before me. In an instant I was back on that yacht. I felt the rocking of the waves and remembered the elation of flying her off the yacht, knowing she at least had a fighting chance. I remembered how tight Anna Crew had hugged me the night before and the gratefulness I could feel in that embrace. I was not finished arguing my case.

"Do you have a daughter, Sir?" I asked, looking up at him.

His eyes squinted at me inquisitively. "Why, yes I do," he replied.

"I'm just asking because I have a sister who is Kirsten Crew's age and I did for Kirsten what I would have done for my sister or your own daughter for that matter. And if..." I took a breath trying to regain my composure, "if the rules have to be bent for the sake of someone else's life then I'm in. And with all due respect Sir, I would do it again if I had to. I thought that was the purpose of a United States Airman. Your willingness to give your life for someone else."

With that I turned on my heel and quickly left the room. I plowed past Mr. Lucas, who didn't try to stop me and I was really grateful for that, but I could see him following me out of the corner of my eye. I walked towards the women's restroom, tears welling up. I had left the meeting quickly, because the last thing I wanted them to see was me crying like a baby.

"*Why was it so easy for some people to not cry?*" I asked myself while the tears flowed freely in the last stall of the bathroom. I hated that I was so sensitive. I stood against the wall talking myself out of crying. I didn't want to come out with my telltale blotchy skin and puffy eyes and let Zhao and the higher ups think I was a wimp, unable to handle the pressures around me.

Outside I heard the bathroom door creak open and soft footsteps walk in.

"Claire?" I heard a kind female voice almost whisper.

"Umm...I'll be right out," I said, trying to pull myself together, then blowing my nose. I straightened my uniform, stuck my chin in the air and attempted to walk confidently out of the stall.

On the other side of the door, Corrin Gray leaned up against the wall, looking sympathetically at me. When I saw her, the lump in my throat immediately returned and I swallowed hard to keep the tears away. She smiled at me, reminding me so much of my mom. Corrin was a bit younger, but just as petite and beautiful, with dark hair and such a kind smile.

"I just wanted to check on you," she said.

"No, I'm fine," my voice cracked and my bottom lip quivered. "*Stop it, Claire.*" I said to myself.

"Yeah ok," she laughed. "Claire, it's ok to cry."

"No it's not," I replied, biting my lower lip as if that would help me.

Corrin wrapped me up in her arms and silently let me cry for the next couple of minutes, then put my face in her hands and made me look at her. "How old are you, Claire?"

"Nineteen."

"Nineteen," she repeated. "You're just a baby. Just because you're an Airman, doesn't mean you're exempt from emotions. What has happened to you merits all the crying and emotions you want to feel. No one on this entire planet understands what you are going through and so far I think you have done an exemplary job of handling this."

I looked at her, surprised by what she had just said to me. No one had ever told me that before. "You do?"

"Absolutely," she smiled. "And you know what else? Lt. General thinks so too."

"He does?" I asked in disbelief. "I thought I was too much of a problem area for him."

"Well, he's a pilot, Claire. He gets it. Do you know what he does on the weekends when he's not working?"

I shook my head no.

"He's flying. I can't keep him grounded for a minute. He's just as addicted as you are, so he understands. He just wants you to be safe...as well as all the uppers. They are all concerned for your safety."

I nodded at her, knowing she was right. "Thank you, Mrs. Gray."

"Corrin. Call me Corrin," she laughed. "Especially since we're going to be roomies for a bit."

"OK Corrin," I smiled back.

"So you pull yourself together and I'll be waiting outside in the hallway for you. You'll be riding home with me and Lt. General tonight.

FIVE

FIFTEEN MINUTES LATER, I sat alone in the back of the Gray's tinted window SUV, enroute back to their home.

"Where's Mr. Lucas?" I asked, looking around and noticing two Military Police vehicles following behind and one in the front of us.

"He got called out on assignment," Lt. General answered, as I noticed him reach across the console and take Corrin's hand. My heart sank and I wished that it were me and Johnny. He always held my hand. No matter where we were or what we were doing, he would always grab my hand and I missed it immensely. "He'll be back though," he reassured me. "We've got it covered."

"I'm going back to Houston, aren't I, Lt. General?"

He sighed, then looked at me in the rearview mirror. "I think so, Claire. It's not that we don't want you here,

42

because believe me, I pushed for them to let us keep you. But this is bigger than anything we could have imagined. Williams showed me data we have received and you are news all over the world now, which means you are in grave danger. You need to be in a secure location."

I sat back in my seat, depression and gloom closing in around me like a thick blanket. "How long do I have?" I asked, as Corrin looked back at me sympathetically.

"Well, like CSM Williams said, maybe two weeks. We don't want to risk anyone seeing you leaving or tracking your flight."

"They have that capability?" Corrin asked in disbelief.

"Honey, they have more capabilities than you can imagine," Lt. General said. "But we're smarter still and we are not going to let anything happen to Claire."

That night I lay in bed, wide awake, staring up at the ceiling. Out of habit, I picked up my phone and dialed Johnny's number. I had to have called it a million times in the last month. It had been weeks since I last heard from him and with all the craziness I had going on, I was expecting to at least get a text from him.

"*Your call can not be completed at this time, please try your call again later,*" the familiar operator's recording sang in my ear. I plugged my phone in the charger and laid down on my pillow again. In the distance I could hear the waves crashing on the beautiful beaches of

Oahu. I dreaded the day I would have to leave Hawaii. I thought about Zhao and my little island and all the guys I worked with. Despite being away from my family, coming to Hickam had been the best thing that happened to me, considering the situation I was in. In my four short months here, I had become quite the little fighter. With all the workouts I had been doing with my specialized fighter group, I had muscles popping through I didn't even know were there. Then Professor Corral had taught me these awesome Jiu Jitsu defense tactics I had become very skilled in. And not to toot my own horn, but I had practiced very hard with Zhao and had easily demolished the two guys who jumped me on the yacht the night I saved Kirsten. (One, I had pretty much rendered unconscious and infertile and the other was probably in a hospital somewhere getting his arm I had cracked backwards and in half, in a cast. I smiled at the thought of that. What a bunch of losers.)

But most of all I would miss my island. My place of escape. What I wouldn't give to be laying on my large flat rock on the south side of the island surrounded by sand, listening to the waves crash around me and watching the shooting stars above that lulled me to sleep so many nights. I felt like it was an old friend, like I couldn't leave Hawaii without saying goodbye, but with all the security I was under that just seemed impossible.

The rest of the weekend I spent hunkered down at the Gray's compound. Zhao was allowed to come and hang out for a while and we spent a lot of time talking, snacking, and watching movies. Zhao was not one to sit and watch TV, so I was more than excited to introduce him to all my 80's favorites he had never seen, including *Back to the Future, Iron Eagle, Pretty in Pink,* and *E.T.* I also taught him to play poker, a game I had learned from the soldiers at the Houston compound. Zhao was such a brainiac, he pretty much had the game figured out by round two and wiped me out of all the peanut M&M's I had bet by the time we were done.

Monday morning I woke early, despite the limited amount of sleep I had got the night before. I was curious to see how my day would go now that my entire schedule had changed.

I got ready and into my uniform, then headed quickly downstairs. Corrin stood at the kitchen counter, looking so cute in her work out clothes. I immediately noticed a bowl of fresh fruit and yogurt sitting on the counter waiting for me.

"Zhao said that was your favorite breakfast food," she explained as she saw me glance over at it.

"Yes Ma'am," I smiled at her.

"Claire, I know you're from the South, but none of that Ma'am stuff is necessary," she laughed.

"Oh, ok." I smiled. That would be a tall order. Since I was from the south, Sir and Ma'am is something we all learned with potty training.

"So, slight change of plans for you," she said, pouring a cup of orange juice. "Adam...excuse me, Lt. General wants you to come straight to his office this morning before you do anything else." Corrin raised her eyebrows and smiled at me with a little, knowing twinkle in her eye, that made me perk up with curiosity.

"Is everything ok?" I asked.

"Oh, yes. Nothing bad, so don't worry."

I finished my breakfast quickly and said goodbye, then jumped in the back seat of an M.P. vehicle waiting outside. This one I noticed, had black tinted windows and we were soon followed closely by an exact replica of it. Ten minutes later we pulled in front of Hickam Headquarters, where I was escorted in by the two M.P.'s.

"Good Morning Haley," Lt. General greeted me, as I entered his office. "Did you sleep well?"

"Yes Sir," I said, standing at attention.

"Good," he replied, walking past me toward the door. "At ease. Follow me, please."

I followed him upstairs and to the end of the hall to a long rectangular room. In it were wall to wall desks with laptops and above them on the south wall, a large screen glowed a bright white.

"Go ahead, Sir." Lt. General instructed the only other person in the room. He then motioned for me to sit at the table directly facing the screen.

Immediately four faces popped on the screen and I gasped at the sight of my mom and my three sisters. In fact, we all gasped with excitement! It had been months since I had seen my baby sister Kass and my mom and almost a year this Christmas since I had seen my two older sisters, Danielle and Tessa.

"Oh my God," I gasped, catching my breath as tears filled my eyes.

"Claire!" They all said at the same time. "It's so good to see you! Are you ok? Did you get hurt? Is everything going ok?" The questions came all at once.

I looked up at them in disbelief. It was hard for me to know what to say. My mom and Kass had known about my flying power for so long, but I never had the chance to tell Tessa and Dani. Tessa and her army husband Ryan, were stationed in Ft. Bragg, while Dani lived the single life in California. I was instructed very clearly that no one was to know about my flying power, not even my sisters. The only reason Kass knew was because she caught me coming back from flying one night and then of course I had to let my mom know. Johnny had been the one who encouraged me to tell her. But I felt terrible not telling Dani and Tessa. I felt like somehow I had betrayed them, even though the situation was out of my hands. I had always told my sisters everything.

I looked back at Lt. General, who stood in the back smiling. "It's ok. You can talk to them about everything. You're on a very secure line."

"Thank you," I said, feeling those two words were not adequate enough for my gratitude.

"You're welcome," he smiled again. "Corrin and I felt like you could use a little pick me up and there's nothing better than a little family time."

I nodded in agreement, blinking back a tear from falling.

"Ok," he said, walking toward the door with the officer right behind him. "We'll give you a little alone time. You have about 30 minutes."

"Thank you, Sir," I said again as the door closed softly behind them. I turned back around to the smiles of four of the most important people in my whole world.

"Aww Claire, don't cry," Tessa said in her usual mommy voice.

I wiped my eyes with my hands. "I'm sorry. I'm just so glad to see you guys. I've been missing you like crazy."

"Oh Claire, we've been missing you too," said Dani. "We've been so worried about you."

"I'm ok, you guys. I'm healthy and everything is as normal as it can be with my body." I looked at my mom, who stared with worry. "Mom, seriously I'm fine," I smiled at her. "I promise. I have my own doctor here and he gave me the all clear yesterday morning."

"Oh I know," my mom said, popping a smile on and trying to reassure me she wasn't worried (even though I could tell she was.) "I completely trust the leadership there, Claire. I know they are taking great care of you."

She was so funny. I could read her like a book. She didn't want me to worry about her worrying about me, so she was playing it cool...if that makes any sense.

"I can't even believe this right now," Tessa almost whispered as if someone were listening. "I can't even believe this is real, Claire."

"I know," I said, biting my lower lip nervously. "I swear you guys, if I could have told you, I would've in a heartbeat."

"We know you would, Claire," Dani said. "Mom and Kass explained everything to us."

"Is that how you found out?" I asked.

"No," said Dani. "I saw it on social media and I did a double take thinking it looked just like you, but Kass called me before it had a chance to register."

"Ryan told me," Tessa smiled. "It's all the talk at Ft. Bragg."

"It's all the talk everywhere!" said Kass. "It's a mad house here in Clarksville."

"Oh," I sighed a little worried. "Well, do they...the people in Clarksville know it's me? I mean, it's not affecting you and mom negatively is it?"

"Oh honey, please don't worry about Kass and I. We're fine. Major Silva has made sure we are good," Mom smiled. I missed her so much.

Kass suddenly sat up straight in her seat, her eyes full of excitement, talking a hundred miles an hour, and as always, exaggerating every word with her hands. "Claire, you should see this place. Everyone is so excited about you, except of course they don't know it's you. They are just excited because after 2 years of rumors of a flying girl, you're a reality now."

"Mom said people are hanging out at places you've been spotted and trying to catch a glimpse of you," Dani laughed, placing her hands on her cheeks, shaking her head in disbelief. "I just can't even believe this is real right now."

"Well, it's not just madness in Clarksville, you have the whole world's attention Claire," Tessa added. "I've seen clips of news reports all over the world, in so many different languages talking about you."

I sat quietly taking in all they were telling me. Here in my little island bubble in the middle of the Pacific, I wasn't hearing too much of the hype happening. Lt. General had only mentioned it briefly, but he didn't say it was this drastic.

"This is insane," I said finally, my eyes wide in disbelief.

"Claire, how is that girl?" Mom asked. "What is her name?"

"Kirsten," I answered. "I think she's going to be ok. Those jerks had her so drugged, it's taken a while for her to come around, but I hear she's getting better."

"What happened Claire?" Kass asked. "Why did you have to save her?"

I paused for a moment, reluctant to tell my story in front of mom. She worried so much about us girls, I didn't want to add to the stress she was probably already feeling.

"Ummm.." I stuttered, trying to figure out how to get the story out, without all the gory details. I would try and sugar coat it the best I could. I spent the next fifteen minutes trying to cover the last four months and what had led up to me having to save Kirsten. My family sat quietly, enthralled in my story and hanging onto every word I said. They gasped when I told them how I had to fight the two creeps on the yacht, (I treaded lightly with mom on that part, making it sound like no big deal) and they laughed when I told them I had stuck my tongue out at the bad guys as I shot off the deck of the yacht with Kirsten. Then came the final scene of me landing on the beach. I did my best to explain everything to them, not skipping a heart stopping detail.

"So Zhao and I didn't realize it, but we had been communicating on the Coast Guard's emergency channel they were using that day. They heard our conversation so when I was flying in with Kirsten, they thought I was an aircraft in distress."

"Oh!" said Tessa. "I was wondering how they knew you were going to land at that airfield."

"Yep," I continued. "So by the time I broke through the clouds with Kirsten, it was too late. We were so cold, she was barely breathing, and I couldn't carry her for one more minute. I had no choice, but to land on the runway, right in the middle of all the first responders."

"Oh my goodness Claire," Kass almost whispered. "That must have been terrifying."

"It was Kass, but I had no choice. If I hadn't got her there when I did, she would have died."

"What happened once you guys landed?" Dani asked.

I was quiet for a moment, remembering the deafening silence despite the chaos all around. "It was weird. It was so quiet for a long moment, I think with just everyone taking in the freak show that I am... and then just a lot of yelling. Some people approached us cautiously with cameras in hand while others ran in fear. That's when Zhao grabbed Kirsten and told me to run."

"Claire," Mom said, her brow furrowed in concern, "You're not a freak show. Why would you say that? You are a walking miracle."

I nodded quietly in agreement, just to make her feel better. "Sometimes, it just seems that way Mom," I shrugged.

They all stared at me concerned, but mom wouldn't let it go. "Claire, I'm sure to the Crew family and Kirsten, you are far from a freak show. Because of you, that young lady is alive and now she has another chance at life."

"Mom is right, Claire." Dani chimed in. "No one thinks bad of you, in fact it's the polar opposite. You are like celebrity superhero status over here."

"And we are all so proud of you," smiled Tessa.

I smiled back at my family. If all else failed in my life, I knew I had them. No matter what I was going through, I knew my sisters always had my back and vice versa. I missed them like crazy.

"Thanks, you guys."

"So have you heard from Johnny?" Kass asked.

I sighed. "No, I was going to ask y'all the same thing. It's been 2 months since I've talked to him."

"Oh Claire, that's completely normal," said Tessa. "When Ryan was in Afghanistan, I went six weeks at one point without hearing anything from him."

That made me feel a little better, but I thought I would have heard from him for sure by now, especially with all that had been going on this past week. I knew he had access to the internet there and if not, Major Silva would have at least reached out to him.

The thirty minutes I had with them passed so quickly. We finished up the conversation with Tessa and Dani asking lots of questions about the accident that caused my superpower and the first few months of flying. I promised to show them some of my flight videos I had recorded and we made a pact to try and spend Christmas together. That was now only three and a half short months away.

Mom prayed over us all, as she always did and we said our "I love you's" before hanging up. At the end, Lt. General joined me and I was able to introduce him to my family. He was very kind and professional to them and I could tell just talking to him immediately put my mom at ease. That made me feel so much better.

"Thank you Lt. General," I said as we walked out to the SUV waiting for us. "That meant the world to me."

"You're very welcome Claire," he smiled. "And just so you know, that call was made possible by CSM Williams." My eyebrows shot up at him in disbelief. I thought CSM Williams was pretty much done with me, especially since my little outburst at our meeting the other day. "I think he likes you a little more than you think."

SIX

THAT WEEK MY everyday schedule went pretty much as follows:

   -An early morning short physical with Major Wang at Tripler Army Medical Center, always with a check of my heart rate and a small blood test.

   -Breakfast at Dillingham airfield with Zhao.

   -Flight testing in the largest hangar at Dillingham with Dr. Zhao.

   -Lunch

   -And finally my favorite, jiu jitsu training with Prof. Braulio Corral at the shack.

Things had changed a lot in my jiu jitsu training. Now that Prof. B knew I could fly, he made a whole new training he called *Voar Jiu Jitsu*, which means air Jiu Jitsu in English. (Zhao shook his head and rolled his eyes

54

laughing when he heard that one.)

"Ok Miss Supergirl," Prof. B said that Friday afternoon as he, Zhao, and I stood on the mat. "This is going to be a little different for you, but no matter what, the same rules of jiu jitsu still apply. Don't forget."

"Yes Sir," I said looking up at his tall 6 foot 3 inch frame. Professor began to explain how all the techniques I have learned can be applied while in the air. He showed me how easy it was to take my opponents back by hovering and slipping past them to a better position. We drilled the coolest jiu jitsu moves, flying triangle chokes, flying armbars, and flying guillotine chokes. These moves are really difficult and are usually attempted by high level, experienced practitioners. I am still a novice but whatever, I can fly so they were pretty easy for me. Professor and I were so excited to see how far we could push my limits now that he knew my secret and how I could use my power to my advantage. But poor Zhao. While limited to the ground, we would have close matches and regularly submit each other. I could see the frustration in him, as he couldn't stop my movement when gravity was not in play for me.

Above all though, the single most important thing Professor taught me about fighting with my superpower is this: you never lose a fight that you don't have. It was simple. If I could fly, I should always fly away from a fight if I have to.

That night I went back to an empty house. Lt. General and Corrine were out for the night at an officer's luau party. Corrine had apologized repeatedly for having to leave me alone, but explained that it was for a dear friend who was retiring and they felt it would be wrong to not attend. I had been given special instructions to stay put and reminded that extra security would be in place outside and inside the house.

I set my duffle bag on the bottom of the staircase and wobbled my way into the kitchen to get a bottle of water. Professor Corral's Voar Jiu Jitsu was kicking my tail and I couldn't wait to get a hot shower and just chill out.

I had just shut the fridge door when the sound of the front door unlocking caught my attention. I immediately flew to the corner of the high ceiling ready to pounce on someone if need be.

"Claire?" I heard a familiar voice call and I immediately jumped down from my position, a little embarrassed by my knee jerk reaction. I peeked around the corner into the entry hall to see a familiar smiling face.

"Sgt. Mancuso!" I exclaimed. "They didn't tell me you would be here!"

Sgt. Mancuso, who seemed genuinely happy to see me again, held up his hand for our usual high five greeting. "Hey! How have you been, little trouble maker?"

I high fived him a little harder than normal, in response to his joke. "Haha," I said dryly. "At least, I'm not boring," I smiled, repeating what Johnny had told me a thousand times, when I had complained about what a pain I was in his life. My tummy twisted in sadness at the thought of Johnny. I missed him more every day.

"Well Miss Excitement," he smirked. "I'm in charge of babysitting you tonight, so don't give me any trouble."

"I'm too pooped for any trouble," I yawned.

"Well, let's keep it that way," he laughed, then pointed toward the kitchen. "Mrs. Gray left dinner on the stove. Are you hungry?"

"I'm always hungry, but I need to shower first." I threw my duffle over my shoulder and headed for the stairs.

"Well make it fast, because I'm starving and that shrimp alfredo is calling my name."

I turned around on the third step up and looked down at him. "You're waiting for me to eat?" I asked, surprised.

"Well yeah," Mancuso said. "I want to hear all about the last two years of your life."

"Ahhh," I said, starting up the steps quickly. "I knew there was a catch."

Thirty minutes later, I sat at the kitchen bar with Sgt. Mancuso, my thick brown spiral curls air drying, eating the best shrimp alfredo I had ever had, while Sinatra's *One For My Baby* played quietly from the kitchen bluetooth speaker.

Sgt. Mancuso stared curiously at my Saturn ring tattoo on my wrist. "So why is it gray now?" he asked.

"Because I haven't been able to fly in a while. It fades

when I'm not flying."

"That is so weird," he said.

"Sgt. Mancuso, my whole life is weird," I laughed.

He smiled, nodding his head agreeing with me. "What does your guy think of all of this?"

"Johnny seems ok with it all, but sometimes I wonder if I'm too much for him. I mean, he's somewhere...I don't even know where or what he's doing..but he has the stress of that and now..now he has to deal with everything going on here with me."

"What is he saying about what happened with Kirsten?"

"I haven't talked to him in almost two months now," I sighed, "So I'm not sure. He's so patient with me though. It becomes too much for me sometimes and then I break it off, but then I can't stay away from him and so we get back together and then I break it off again and he just patiently waits for me to come back each time." I paused for a moment, realizing I had said too much. "I'm sorry Sgt. Mancuso. TMI, I know."

"It's ok, Claire," he smiled. "Let me tell you something about guys. If we care about you, we'll wait. We'll wait through all the confusion and all the unknown. It sounds like he really loves you, so nothing, even the craziness of all this can stop that."

"Seriously?" I asked.

"Seriously," he repeated confidently.

I smiled at Sgt. Mancuso, remembering my first encounter with him. As my commanding officer he came across as this brute of a man, but I had come to

58

realize the civilian in him was just this giant teddy bear.

I raised an eyebrow at him. "If you know so much about relationships, why are you still single?"

"Married to the job Claire," he laughed pointing at his ring finger. "Married to the job."

We spent the next hour talking about my flying adventures. I told him how I had secretly helped the police at home catch criminals and how I had been arrested breaking into the hangar at Ft. Campbell trying to get the rest of the pink flying potion. He sat on the edge of his seat for that conversation, asking a lot of questions. This poor guy was begging for conversation. I'm pretty sure out of everyone I had told my story to, he had the most questions.

I yawned as the clock in the kitchen chimned 9 p.m. I had a feeling he could have talked a while longer, but he recognized the heaviness in my eyes.

"Get to bed girl," he said, taking our plates to the kitchen sink. "And don't worry about anything. I'm right here if you need me."

I slid slowly down from the bar stool. "Thank you Sgt. Mancuso. It was nice talking to you."

"It was nice talking to you too...and Claire," he said pointing his finger at me, "If you ever need anything at all, you know where I'm at."

I lay in bed that night unable to sleep, despite the

exhaustion I was feeling. I knew that in just a few days my life would change drastically again with the move to Houston and the dread clutched my spirit, making me feel like I was dragging an actual weight around.

Around eleven, I heard the Grays come home and Sgt. Mancuso leaving. A short time later I saw a shadow pause by the bottom crack under my door. I assumed it was Corrin checking on me to see if I was ok. I appreciated her respect for my privacy by not opening the door, so I coughed to assure her I was in my bed where I should be.

My Saturn tattoo glowed a warm pink from underneath the covers. "No, I'm not flying tonight," I whispered to my tat, as if it had a mind of its own and could understand what I was saying. I stared down at it. Well, maybe it could understand me, because suddenly it seemed to glow even brighter in protest.

Something I think people don't understand about my flying power is this: I need to fly. In fact, my body craves it. And when I say need, I mean that as in a physical necessity. It's almost like an itch I can't scratch and it just drives me crazy until finally I can't take it anymore and I will do whatever I can to get into the air.

I was very much feeling that itch tonight. I lay in bed until almost three imagining myself high above the Pacific. I would be looking down at the beautiful lights of Oahu, sparkling off the dark, mysterious rolling waves. Then I would flip over and watch the thousands of diamond stars glittering against the black sky, with the occasional bright orange streak of a shooting star catching my eye.

I needed to fly again. What's more, I needed to fly to my island. I needed to say goodbye.

SEVEN

A BRIGHT SATURDAY sun filled my room and my eyes popped open. I rolled over in bed and took a deep breath. Something was different. My body felt different. My mind felt clearer. For days I had been waking up in a daze, but today I felt energized, like I had been asleep for months.

I jumped out of bed and threw on my flannel pajama pants, then headed downstairs. Corrin sat at the kitchen bar drinking coffee and reading a news site on her computer. She glanced up at me, cocking her head sideways and looking me over curiously.

"You look really chipper today," she laughed.

"Thank you," I smiled, taking a banana out of the fruit bowl and peeling it. "I feel really chipper today. Very well rested."

"Well, you should," she said, nodding toward the clock on the wall. "It's almost noon."

My eyes grew wide, slightly embarrassed by my laziness. "Oh wow," I smiled.

"It's ok...you needed it," she winked, patting me on the back. "I was thinking about changing into my swimsuit and catching some rays for a bit. Care to join me?"

"Sure," I replied, thinking about how I needed to swim some laps anyway. Without my regular PT exercises, I was feeling pretty out of shape and frumpy.

I threw my banana peel in the garbage and headed upstairs, quickly changing into my bikini and a cover up. By the time I got down to the pool, Corrin was already poolside in one of the lounge chairs looking so adorable in her black bikini and now reading off an Ipad.

"*Wow, I hope I can still rock a two piece when I'm in my forties,*" I thought as I parked myself in the lounge chair beside her.

"Where is Lt. General today?" I asked, looking around the tidy back yard for him, before I took off my cover up.

Corrin peaked out from under her shades and matching sun hat. "Remember when I told you I couldn't keep him out of the sky?"

I smiled knowing where she was going with this.

"He should be flying over any minute now."

I giggled. "Oh, how I know that feeling. I wanted so badly to fly last night."

Corrin put down her Ipad and looked at me sympathetically. "I can't imagine having such a wonderful gift and never getting to use it."

"Oh Corrin, you have no idea," I said, turning to her. "Last night the urge to fly was so overwhelming. Like, my body literally *craves* it."

Corrin was quiet for a moment and then sighed. "I wish there was something I could do to help you Claire, but it's just too unsafe right now." She pointed down at the Ipad. "I was reading about you online, just to see what's going on outside of Hawaii and you are just...just everywhere."

I nodded in agreement, "That's what I heard."

I layed back in my chair and we were silent for a moment, enjoying the sounds of the tropical birds and bubbling of the water in the pool. I breathed in the salt water air, soaking in the moment, because I knew in just 6 short days I would be on my way to the dry desert air of Texas.

The humming of an airplane broke the tropical symphony and Corrin immediately sat up in her seat.

"I think that's him," she smiled. "Every Saturday at 12:30."

I looked up into the clear sky and saw a small twin engine plane approaching our air space, its yellow belly a stark contrast to the bright blue behind it. Lt. General guided the plane directly over us, slowly dropping a bit as the engine grew louder. Corrin and I waved as big as we possibly could, in hopes that he might somehow see us. In my mind, I imagined how great it would be to pop in the air and wave as he flew right by me. I smiled so big, waving once again, my eyes full of envy. I watched until he was no longer anything, but a small dark speck. What a lucky guy.

I turned my attention back to earth and looked at Corrin, who was staring at me with sympathy in her eyes.

"You're the most pitiful thing I think I've ever seen," she laughed, as we both sat back down. "You're drooling a bit there."

I covered my face, blushing in my embarrassment. I really liked Corrin Gray. She was just enough to be part mother, part friend. "I'm so sorry," I giggled.

She was quiet for a moment, then a mischievous grin slowly formed on her perfect little lips. "You know Claire, it's supposed to be clear tonight and Lt. General is usually a heavy sleeper."

My mouth gaped open slightly, unsure if she was saying what I thought she was saying. My face lit up as I looked at her inquisitively. "You mean..?"

"I'm just saying," she interrupted before I could question her further, "Adam doesn't hear anything when he sleeps and I usually check on everyone before I go to bed... and then again around 4."

I smiled at her, knowing "everyone" meant me, since I was the only other person in the house. I couldn't even wrap my mind around what I was hearing. Corrin was giving me the ok to fly tonight.

That whole day completely dragged, despite the fun I had with Corrin hanging out by the pool and helping her cook dinner. We talked about everything and I was completely enthralled in her story and how she met Lt. General.

"So, you were in the Air Force and he was your boss too?" I asked, as we cut up vegetables for dinner.

"Yep," she smiled. "It was a hard decision for me. I dreamed of being in the Air Force my whole life, just like my dad. After my four years were up, I had to decide what I wanted more; a life with Adam Gray or my military career."

"I can't imagine how hard that must have been," I sighed. "What a sacrifice you made."

"Well, if you love someone deep enough, you will move heaven and earth to be with that person and I loved Adam so much, it wasn't hard letting it go."

I looked out the window as one of the guards outside casually walked by, scanning the west side of the house. I thought about Johnny and how I could definitely relate to Corrin sacrificing something she loved so much for Lt. General. I would give up my flying power in an instant to be with Johnny forever.

"You ok?" She asked, snapping me out of my thoughts.

"Oh yeah. I'm fine," I blushed.

"What's his name?" she asked knowingly. I looked at her surprised. This woman was so much like my mom. She could read me like a book. "Come on, what's his name?"

I took a deep breath. "Johnny," I said exhaling. "Johnny Angel."

"Johnny Angel?" she asked as if she didn't believe me.

"Yes," I giggled. "I know, I know."

"Where is he?"

I took another deep breath. "Somewhere in Afghanistan."

Her eyes sank. "Oh Claire, I can't imagine how hard that must be for you. Does he know...?"

"Yes," I interrupted her. "I mean, he knows I can fly... but as far as everything that has happened these past two weeks, I'm not sure. I have a feeling he doesn't though, because if he did, I know I would have heard from him already."

She nodded in agreement with me. "Well, when Adam was over there I didn't hear from him for almost a month. I'm sure as soon as he can, he will get in touch with you."

I smiled at her, attempting to hide the mix of emotions I was feeling. I definitely wanted to hear from him, but at the same time, I hoped he had no clue about what happened here. I didn't want to add to his stress anymore.

That night, I excused myself to go to bed early.

"Well, you're not much of a night owl," Lt. General teased me. "It's only 8:30, Haley."

"I know," I smiled, "but I think all that sun today got to me."

Lt. General laughed. "I think we all know what got to you. Corrin wears me out too."

Corrin rolled her eyes smiling, while I giggled and turned to head upstairs.

"Oh Claire," she called after me.

I turned around halfway up. "Yes Ma'am?"

"Sweet dreams," she winked, while I nodded knowingly at her.

Upstairs, I quickly brushed my teeth and layed out my clothes I would be wearing later in the night. That afternoon, I had walked the property and devised a quick plan to make my getaway a little more easy. Lucky for me, there were plenty of full palm trees to hide in, all the way off the property. I would go from tree to tree, until at last I hit the beach and then rocket into the air from there.

I layed down thinking I would be too excited to sleep, but my body sank into the soft mattress and I could feel drowsiness sweeping over me. I quickly set my alarm for 1:30 in anticipation of being in the air by 2 and before I knew it, I drifted into a deep sleep.

EIGHT

BOBBY DARIN'S *"SOMEWHERE Beyond The Sea,"* played softly in my ear, waking me from my sleep coma. I rolled over and looked at my phone as I shut it off. One thirty. No need to collect my thoughts on why I was waking so early. I was flying tonight! I hadn't flown in over two weeks and was so excited I was shaking.

I jumped up and threw on my clothes, making sure I was completely dressed in black. I couldn't believe Corrin was letting me do this and I wondered why she had changed her mind so fast. I must have looked really pathetic earlier when we were talking about it.

"Claire, promise me you'll be back no later than 4," she had reminded me.

"I promise," I had said. *"Corrin, I can't thank you enough. This means the world to me."*

I smiled as I laced up my black Chucks, pulled my long curls into a high ponytail, stuffed my covers with my duffle bag, then pulled my hoodie up and grabbed my phone. I paused quietly in my room, listening to make sure everyone was sound asleep. Outside the wind blew lightly and the tall palm just outside my window whistled softly in the breeze. That was my first target.

I peeked out from the lace curtains to an empty yard below, on the west side of the house. There were always two guards on duty. One guarded the front and one on the back and they switched positions every thirty minutes. I felt so sorry for them. They must have been bored out of their minds and wondered what in the world they were doing guarding Lt. General's house.

When the coast was clear, I gently unlocked the window, slowly slid it open and crept out onto the window sill. The palm tree was just 10 feet away. I set my sights on the large palm branches, then as quick as an eye blink flew up and under the palm umbrella, tucking myself out of sight. The wind again blew calmly through the palms, making a loud whisping noise. I had just turned to fly to the next tree when something white caught my eye. The lace curtain had been sucked out of the window I had left open and was now blowing erratically in the warm breeze. To make matters worse, a guard turned the corner and was now headed down my side of the house. How could I have been so careless? One look at that open window and I was so busted.

The guard came closer and I panicked at the thought

of him seeing the open window. I had to find a way to distract him. I grabbed an apple from my backpack and quickly tossed it behind him into the bushes. Thankfully I had a pretty good arm and it hit the tall fence that surrounded the property, making a loud thudding sound. He immediately turned to investigate.

Meanwhile, I pushed off the side of the tree and glided softly through the air and back into the window bringing the curtains in with me. Using two plastic hoops that hang on either side of the window, I secured them in place and then peeked out of the window to see if the guard was still distracted. I could barely see him in the moonlight, his flashlight frantically scanning the area back and forth. Poor guy. I didn't mean to freak him out.

I climbed back out onto the window and slid it quietly down, leaving it barely cracked for easy access later. Getting from one tree to the other was no problem now that both guards were busy searching that side of the house. I followed the treeline of palms all the way down to the beach, then jumped onto the white sand below to eyeball the area from the ground. Sometimes when I launched from a high level, I took for granted the fact that there could be people below me, unseen from my height and I didn't want to make that mistake. When the coast was all clear, I popped my earbuds in and Phil Collins' *In the Air Tonight,* muffled the sound of the crashing waves. I looked into the majestic star filled sky above me and shot off the sand like a rocket. One hundred feet, two hundred, three hundred and fifty feet flew by quickly. My speed felt so much stronger tonight. Once I felt a safe distance offshore, I would drop to the surface of the water and do what we in the Air Force call *Nap Of the Earth* flying, which basically means we fly close to the surface to avoid radar detection.

At 500 feet, I felt secure enough to head southwest toward my island. It was so beautiful tonight. The wind was calm and the moon so bright. Below I could see the white caps of waves rolling endlessly toward Oahu and a flock of tropical cranes flying to the northwest. I adjusted my small backpack and flipped on my back to see if I would be lucky enough to catch a shooting star. Tonight was pretty clear, but at one point I did see a jet high above me. That reminded me to drop to the ocean surface and fly there the rest of the way.

At last the waves breaking against the rocky side of my island appeared in the distance. I looked at my watch. It had only taken me 30 minutes to get here, instead of my usual 40 to 45. I felt a little emotional as I flew over the cliffs and onto the sandy beach side, where my large flat rock awaited my landing. Just to be safe though, I circled the island checking for anything foreign or out of place. When everything looked good, I landed softly on my rock and dropped my backpack, then paused to enjoy this beautiful moment. The waves crashed endlessly against the beach and an occasional tropical bird cawed in the distance. I wiped a tear from my eye. I thought I would never see my island again and I blinked to make sure I wasn't dreaming. Corrin was my life saver and I knew I could never thank her enough. I had spent so much of yesterday talking about my island to her, I decided to take some video of it tonight so she could see how amazing it is.

I slid off my shoes and started recording, while walking the beach narrating every beautiful step on the white sand. The moonlight shone against its sparkle and despite the dark sky, it illuminated the island in a natural light. "Corrin, this is my island..." I began, as I started the tour.

I walked her around to the north side of the island, which only took about 15 Minutes, since my island was relatively small.

"And there's the cave I was telling you about," I said pointing my phone toward the dark hole in the rock wall, a little bit up from the beach. "That's where I first saw the drug smugglers. They were right here on this beach." I then took to the sky to give her a view of the cliffs, eventually flying around the whole perimeter of the island.

When I finally finished, I decided to walk back around the beach again, instead of flying over the tropical garden that separated the north side from the south. Michael Buble's "*Home*" played gently from my iPod as the wind blew steadily from the west. I paused for a moment on the furthest point of the west beach and allowed the salt air and spray to wash over me. I stared into the watery darkness and thought of my Johnny. I wondered where he was on this night and if he was ok. I would give anything to be able to bring him to this island and spend time alone with him. Just me and him and no one else in the whole world. I would have him all to myself away from friends, family, the military and the nosey media.

At last I headed back down the beach, making a quick stop at one of my favorite palm trees that canopied over the sand from the tropical rainforest to the ocean. There was one thing I had been wanting to do before I left for a while. I took a small knife out of my front pocket and began carving slowly and meticulously, so I got it just right. When I was done, I stepped back and observed my handiwork. I smiled as I read "C loves J" surrounded by a perfectly shaped heart, then took out my phone to snap a pic so I could show Johnny.

I made it back to my rock that had sometimes doubled as a bed and layed down using my backpack as a pillow. The waves softly rolled in as I watched the stars slowly pass above. I blinked hard, reminding myself not to fall asleep. *(Could you imagine the horror I would face tomorrow if I accidentally dozed off? I could just see it now; Corrin would wake up terrified that she could not find me. Lt. General would then put the base on full alert, thinking I had been kidnapped by some foreign government, while Zhao, Professor Corral, and Sgt. Mancuso would be out looking for me. Corrin at last, would be forced to tell him the truth and who knows what it would do to their seemingly perfect marriage? Even worse for me, I would lose Corrin as a friend.)* Anyway, that was enough to keep me wide awake and all too soon it was time for me to fly back.

I stood up and gathered my stuff, then took one last glance around the island. God only knew when I would be back again *but,* I determined in my mind as I shot off the rock and into the sky, I would be back.

NINE

CORRIN SMILED KNOWINGLY at me, as I entered the kitchen the next morning. I had made it safely back to Oahu and into my bedroom window without one ounce of trouble.

"Good morning sleepyhead," she smiled as Lt. General looked up from the newspaper he was reading.

"Good morning," I smiled back as I sat beside them at the counter. "I'm sorry I slept so long," I said sheepishly, glancing up at the kitchen clock that read 10:05.

Lt. General put his paper down. "Well Haley, Major Wang said it will be a bit before you get your energy back to one hundred percent, so it's understandable. Since it's Sunday, you just get a lot of rest. This week you'll be with Prof. Corral and Zhao. We want you to get all the training you can with him while he's here."

That piqued my curiosity. "While he's here?" I asked. "Is he going somewhere?"

"Yep," Lt. General said, taking one more sip of coffee and tucking his newspaper away. "He'll be heading back to Indiana next week."

"Indiana? I repeated, surprised. "You mean he doesn't live here?"

"Oh no," he replied, picking up his plate and walking it to the sink. "He was brought here especially for you. His life is in Northwest Indiana. He has a few academics there."

"Especially for me?" I asked, shaking my head in surprise. "Why?"

"Because Claire, we knew you would need the best ground training we could get you and as you have learned, Professor Corral is the best."

I nodded my head in agreement. He was definitely right about that. My ground fighting abilities in the last 6 months went from non-existent to purple belt status. Professor Corral had told me that if I were in a regular non-military learning status, I would be killing all of the blue and purple belts. For some reason jiu jitsu had come so naturally for me. I'm not sure exactly why that was, but I did know most of it was because of Professor Corral and also because I knew that having this skill could save my life or even more importantly my family's lives if need be. I worked so hard to learn it and it had paid off in my plight to save Kirsten.

"Did you know Professor Corral is going back to Indiana?" I asked Zhao Monday morning as we sat in the back of the SUV on our way to the Shack.

"Yeah, I knew he would be going back, but I didn't think it would happen so soon," Zhao replied.

"Zhao!" I exclaimed. "You knew about him leaving and you didn't tell me?"

Zhao shrugged, "I'm sorry Claire, I just found out last week myself and then when everything went down with you, I forgot."

"All this time, I thought he lived here. I had no idea that he came all the way from Indiana just for...for..."

"For you," Zhao finished for me. "Why else would the guy leave his home and family and agree to live thousands of miles away for some of the year?"

"That doesn't make me feel any better Zhao," I laughed.

Zhao put his arm around me. "Oh Claire, don't stress it. You can tell the Professor is enjoying himself."

We turned onto the brick drive and through the gate marked in big red letters,

"RESTRICTED FACILITY"

Zhao yawned and stretched as I glanced out the back window at the gate closing behind us and the guard making sure it was secure. To the left, I could see a small crew of lawn workers in their matching brown shorts and green tee shirts, cleaning up the dried palm trees that had fallen on the perfectly manicured lawn. Hickam kept this place immaculate.

We pulled up to the front of the building and walked through the lobby to the back of the building and out into the garden. At the end of the path sat the Shack, a smaller building, with a bamboo structure appearance. Zhao and I were greeted at the door as usual by Prof. Corral who was always genuinely glad to see us.

"Good Morning Airmen," he said, echoing his everyday greeting.

"Good Morning Professor," Zhao and I said in unison.

Professor Corral clapped his hands together, "You guys get stretched out, we got a busy morning ahead of us."

Zhao and I stretched immediately, then got to work. Professor Corral continued to push ground combat with me, but we really focused on the new air techniques. I loved using flying triangle chokes. Zhao was more than happy to help and was even forgiving when I accidently turned too quickly from a spin in the air, catching him in the ear with my knee.

By ten o'clock Zhao and I were dripping with sweat and Professor Corral allowed us a ten minute break. Zhao and the Professor headed off to the break room while I, as usual, stepped outside the back door to try and text Johnny. It was midnight in Afghanistan and I always tried to text him late at night there because the last two times I had heard from him was after ten. Somehow I hoped that he would get my message, though I seriously doubted it. I hadn't heard from him in weeks.

"Hi Johnny. I doubt you'll get this, but I thought I would try anyway. I just want you to know that I miss you so much. I pray for your safety everyday and I can't wait until I see you again. PS- don't believe everything you hear in the media. Please talk to me first. I love you-Claire Bear."

I pushed send, then watched as my phone did its usual search thing. I could tell it wasn't going anywhere. I sighed as the sound of a stick cracking to my left caught my attention and out of the corner of my eye I saw one of the lawn guys approach me.

"Excuse me Ma'am," he smiled. "Can I ask you a question?"

"Sure," I said.

I waited as the man continued to smile in silence and walk towards me, while a creepy uneasiness filled my senses. This feeling was all too familiar. The same creepy feeling I had two years ago when I was followed home by the scruffy guys the night I learned I could fly. I watched him closely as he came near. Suddenly I felt a presence behind me as someone in one quick move, covered my head and pulled my arms behind my back. I started to scream, but a hand pushed the cloth from the bag into my mouth. I began kicking as hard as I could and punched the heel of my foot into the man's shin. I heard him grunt in pain, but that was all in vain as the other guy grabbed my legs and they began running with me around the building. I knew exactly where they were going. They would put me in their work van and leave back through the gate unnoticed before anyone would know I was gone.

In that moment, I could remember everything I had been told the last two years. Major Silva and General Collins, my command at Ft.Campbell, CMS Bryant and Commander Whitley at the compound in Houston, and finally Lt. General Gray and CSM Williams here in Hawaii...all of their voices and warnings echoed in my ears at once. They had warned me of this possibility and I gasped in disbelief that it was actually happening.

I started to panic, trying to catch my breath through the cloth in my mouth, then Professor Corral's voice echoed in my head. *"Remember your training. Use what you know."*

I immediately began to squirm with all my might as I felt them round the last corner of the building. I tried desperately to get my legs out of his grasp and managed to get one on the ground. When the guy bent over to grab it, I pushed my leg into the air hoping to connect somewhere and gasped with relief when I felt something on his face crack against my knee.

"You little..." he said, striking me in the face and calling me every name in the book, but was soon interrupted by another grunt. The first guy dropped my shoulders to the ground with a thud and I heard scuffling all around me. I ripped off the cloth sack and looked up. We were just feet from their white van. My eyes grew wide as I watched Professor Corral push the first guy against the van, then take him to the ground with a leg sweep, after softening him up with a short right backfist to his jaw. Behind me freshly laid mulch began flying everywhere after Zhao took the second guy down with an inside trip and fell into a mount position on top of him. Zhao began raining elbow strikes to the guy's face. Watching Zhao demolish this guy was unreal. He had to have been twice the size of Zhao.

I glanced over to see Professor Corral standing on the guy's hand. "Knife! Knife!" he yelled, pinning it against the ground with his foot. The guy screamed in pain as I heard bones cracking in his hand. I quickly got up, grabbing my bruised ribs that were now throbbing in pain and ran to the large knife, kicking it far away from the two. Within minutes both Zhao and the Professor had the men under control, while in the distance I heard the gate guards running toward us.

"Who are you working with?" Zhao yelled, slamming the guy's head in the ground. "Who?!"

The guys remained silent while one of the security guards ran over and rescued him from the beating Zhao was delivering. Zhao had gone from Jiu Jitsu mode to full on street fighter. The guards yanked the men off the ground and then walked them to the back seats of their squads. I looked them over carefully, while wiping blood from my split lip. They didn't look like spies. They both seemed like your average Joes. One was a plain everyday white guy who looked like he could have gone to high school with me back home, while the other looked like a local native Hawaiian. I would have never in a million years thought anything suspicious of them. They knew who I was though and the white guy stared at me with an angry gaze from the back window as he screamed about his severely broken hand. Professor Corral looked at Zhao and I and smirked, "If someone pulls a weapon on you, you make sure they only do it once."

"Message received Sir," Zhao nodded.

"Zhao, walk Claire to the shack with him," Professor Corral said, pointing to a guard who had his weapon drawn. "Stay there until you are instructed further."

Zhao wrapped his arm around me and we walked in stunned silence back to the Shack. Once inside, the security guard checked the building, then locked the door behind us. Zhao and I stood face to face staring at each other. Each breath I took was shallow and the whole inside of my body trembled in fear.

"Are you ok, Claire?" Zhao asked, moving a loose strand of curl out of my eyes. "I swear, I could have killed that guy."

"Zhao?" I gasped. "I can't...how could this have even happened?"

Zhao shrugged his shoulders. I could tell he was just as shaken as I was, "I don't know, Claire. I don't know, but I promise we'll find out."

That night I sat at the Gray's kitchen table, relieved that

I had been brought back here. When the Military Police showed up to retrieve Zhao and I, I thought for sure they would take me straight to the brigade until further notice. Lt. General, Corrin, Professor Corral and Zhao all sat with me, while Major Wang checked my side.

"Well, nothing appears to be any worse," Major Wang said looking at me, then turned his attention to Lt. General. "But still, she needs to stop by Tripler tomorrow and get an xray to be sure."

"Not happening," Lt. General said stiffly. "Claire will be leaving on a midnight flight off the island."

I heard Zhao gasp quietly, the way only I could notice. Zhao was so good at hiding his emotions, but as for me, mine marched right out on my sleeve for all to see. I gasped and then sighed loudly, my disappointment causing tears to pool in the corner of my eyes. Lt. General softened his glare on me a bit.

"I'm so sorry Claire, but we have no other choice. We have those two guys in interrogation right now and they swear they are just a couple of surfers from the mainland who were talked into this for a significant amount of money. We still have no idea who we are dealing with. It's just not safe enough here for you anymore."

I nodded my head agreeing with him because I knew he was right. I knew I had to leave...and not for my safety, but for the safety of others here that I cared about. I definitely couldn't stay in the Grays' home anymore and put them at risk and that went for Zhao and Professor Corral too. Even though they held their own today, it was my fault they were even put in that position in the first place.

Professor Corral put his hand on my shoulder. "I hate to see you go Claire, but Lt. General is right. The fact that those guys or whoever they are working for know who you are and where to find you is a problem."

"There has to be a leak somewhere on the inside," Zhao said, clenching his teeth in anger. "There's no way they could have known anything about Claire being at the Shack. Very few people even know it exists."

"Exactly Zhao," agreed Lt. General. "I trust you gentlemen with everything inside of me, but at this moment everyone's a suspect. For right now the best thing for Claire to do is go into hiding for a while." Then he turned to me. "Claire, you have an hour. Lucas is enroute here to escort you out."

"Yes Sir," I agreed, quietly. I was too exhausted from everything going on to beg them to let me stay. "Come on Zhao. You can help me pack."

Zhao followed me up the winding staircase to my room. We walked in and he closed the door behind me.

"Come here," he said.

I walked into his open arms and the tears began to flow. Zhao said nothing, but held me for a long time. It had been a long day, a long 4 months for that matter. I had come so far here and I didn't want to leave. I especially didn't want to leave Zhao. He was more than my friend, he was my kindred spirit. Do you know what a kindred spirit is? If you don't know, then more than likely you've never had one. A kindred spirit is someone you connect with on every level of your being; socially, emotionally, spiritually. It's meeting someone for the first time, but feeling like you've known them your whole life. I've had very few connections like that in my life. Family excluded, it's been Alicia definitely, Johnny deeply, and now my Zhao. I think it would be much easier leaving tonight, if I had never met him.

When my tears slowed down, he pulled back and took my face in his hands, softly wiping the wet tears off my cheeks.

"Zhao, I don't know how to say goodbye to you. I don't know how I would have made it here without you."

"Same Claire...but don't worry. I was just thinking about everything and I don't see them sending you away and not letting me come. The whole point in me coming here was to help figure you out."

My eyes lit up. "You really think so?"

"Definitely. I think at this point they are just trying to get you somewhere safe and then they'll send me and my dad to help you there."

I nodded my head in agreement because that made sense. I reached up to hug my sweet friend. "Please try and come find me," I whispered to him.

Zhao hugged me tightly. "I promise Claire. I will."

TEN

THE ENGINES OF the small private Air Force jet whined loudly into the quietness of the midnight hour. Mr. Lucas and I were on the backside of Hickam tucked into our seatbelts awaiting clearance from the tower for take off. I looked solemnly outside my small airplane window soaking in the last glimpse I would get of Oahu. Outside at least a dozen MP vehicles surrounded the plane, their lights blacked out to avoid any attention to our departure. In the past I would have thought that was overkill, but after today I was secretly glad they were here.

Mr. Lucas got up and went to the cockpit, tapping lightly on the door to speak with the flight crew. This was his third time up there and I couldn't help but wonder why he had to ask so many questions. When we boarded the flight, both pilots had to show Mr. Lucas their military credentials and be cleared on the tarmac with Lt. General.

My mind went back to just 20 minutes ago as I said my goodbyes to Lt. General. *"You know Haley, if I could keep you here safely, I would,"* he had said.

"I know you would, Sir," I replied, trying to manage a smile. *"I definitely understand why and I appreciate your concern for my safety."*

"They're doing one last inspection underneath and we'll be on our way," Mr. Lucas said, snapping me back into the present.

I nodded my head and leaned back into my seat, covering myself with my favorite blanket from home. My mom had sent me this blanket back at the end of the summer when I was feeling homesick. I was especially glad to have it now.

Twenty minutes later we were taxiing down the runway and then my favorite part, the inertia of being rocketed from the ground, the best feeling ever. We leveled off as I felt the exhaustion of today finally catching up. What a long day it had been. It didn't seem like this morning I was laying on the ground in severe pain, as I watched Professor Corral and Zhao take on those losers. That seemed like a lifetime ago.

A phone ringing broke the heavy silence between Mr. Lucas and I. I watched as he picked up an old school looking phone that hung on the wall by the fire extinguisher. That was so weird. Could those things even work at this height?

"Lucas," he said, identifying himself, then paused as the other person spoke. "Yes Sir," he continued, "we are about 15 minutes into flight...right, I'll have her there around 6 am. Thank you, Sir."

I watched as he hung up the phone, then looked over at me. I didn't even have to ask. "Chief Master Sergeant Bryant," he said. "He'll be meeting us at the compound in the morning."

"I assumed so," I said, smiling slightly at him. "I'm so sorry Mr. Lucas."

"What are you sorry for?" he asked, popping his usual toothpick in his mouth and leaning back in his chair.

"Just because...I don't know. I'm thinking you have more important things to do than babysit me."

"Claire, we've had this discussion before. You are as important a mission to me as anyone or anything else I've ever done."

I smiled to myself. Mr. Lucas was always so kind and gracious to me. His answer piqued my curiosity though. "Mr. Lucas, is it ok if I ask you about what else you've done?" I asked, using my fingers as quotations on the "*what else you've done*" part.

"Well, that depends on what you want to know," he chuckled.

"You know what I mean," I laughed. "What's your story? What brought you into this line of work and what *exactly* do you do?"

Mr. Lucas rolled his eyes, "Oh Claire, it is too late for this sweetie."

"Well...you know my secret," I pleaded.

Mr. Lucas turned his head and looked over at me amused. "Ok," he sighed after a moment. "What do you want to know?"

"Hmmm..." I said, then shrugged my shoulders. "Start from the beginning."

Mr. Lucas settled back in his chair and began his story; Charles Jermaine Lucas was born into a well-to-do family in the autumn of 1979. His father was at one point a pro baseball player and had served in Vietnam and his grandfather in World War II, so it was only natural that he would join the military also. He left home for the Army at the young age of 18, fresh out of high school and was stationed at my homebase, Ft. Campbell, (which I thought was a pretty cool coincidence!) He served 4 tours in Afghanistan and soon was asked to join the elite Army force known as "Special Forces Operational Detachment-Delta."

"Well, I was there for a few years when me and a few buddies of mine were called out one night on a special mission. One of our top commanders at a nearby base in Afghanistan had been ambushed in a motorcade. Everyone was killed but him and he was being held hostage somewhere. We were briefed on where they thought he might be and were told to do overnight surveillance just in case he was moved. Around 3 am I noticed movement in front of the building as they were trying to sneak him out. Well...let's just say they didn't get far." He stared off past me for a moment, deep in thought. "They drove close to our location and I don't know...I just saw red and tore into them. I was so mad at what they had done to my brothers. Anyway, we were able to take out the occupants of the vehicle and get the commander out safely. The next week I got notice to report to the Pentagon, where I was assigned to a top secret government agency." He shrugged as if it were no big deal. "That's about it."

"Were your other buddies asked to join?" I asked.

"Nope, just me."

"Why not them?"

"Because, I guess they liked my aim better."

My eyes grew wide. "Ohhhh..."

Mr. Lucas laughed at me. "You better get some sleep Airman Haley."

"No wait," I said. I was more curious now. "So now you do secret missions for the military?"

He gave me a long side look, like he didn't want to answer at first. "Well, the military and other agencies."

"There's other agencies?" I asked. He just shrugged at me again. "Who would you work for other than the military? What other agencies and what do you do?"

"I just do what they tell me, Claire. If I have to fight, I fight, but mostly it's just escorts like this."

I was really curious now. "Who do you escort? People like me?"

"No one like you, but people, important documents, objects, government...government, I don't know...secrets, experiments."

"Experiments like me?" I smiled.

"You're not an experiment Claire," he said firmly. "You were just in the wrong place at the wrong time...but you're definitely one of the coolest government secrets I've ever had to escort."

"Thank you," I smiled, sticking my chin in the air a little too proud.

"Ok, is that all?" he asked, stretching his long legs out in front of him.

"One more," I insisted. "What is the coolest thing you've ever had to escort... besides me?"

He sighed, clearly amused by my question. "Ahhh man. You had to go there."

"Come on Mr. Lucas, I won't tell. I promise."

"Claire, let me just say this; secrets are secrets for a reason. Sometimes, things are better left unknown." He lowered his voice and his eyes grew serious. "You know how your superpower is not of this world?" I nodded yes. "Well, I've seen the same. Humans would like to think they can handle the unknown, but they can't. Look how stupid they are acting over you."

I nodded my head again in agreement. He was right about that. I had just checked online last night and the Ohau Supergirl had reached a fever pitch and was continuing to grow worldwide.

"Alright now. Let's get some sleep," Mr. Lucas said with a big yawn, reaching for our usual fist bump.

"Ok," I said, fist bumping him back. "Thank you Mr. Lucas."

"Not a problem, girl."

He leaned back and closed his eyes. I had a ton more questions, but knew I should probably let him get some sleep. Poor guy. I bet this was only one of the few times he felt like he could let his guard down, rocketing thousands of feet above the face of the earth.

I leaned my plush leather seat back and snuggled into my blanket, but I couldn't go to sleep. My mind was too full. Mr. Lucas had it racing. I stared over at him sleeping and wondered what other agencies out there existed. Did he mean like a *Men In Black* kind of thing? And what did he mean when he said he had seen things that are not of this world and that humans couldn't handle it? Did he mean aliens or something like that?

I didn't blame him for not telling me anything, because after all, my life was one big secret, but man was this frustrating. I really wanted to know for my own selfish reasons. Maybe if I knew some of what Mr. Lucas knew it could open some doors as to where the pink potion came from. It obviously wasn't from anything earth could produce or we would have already found more. I wanted answers and hoped this next chapter in my life would finally give them to me.

The whining of the jet's engines on approach woke me from my peaceful sleep. My eyes squinted as a bright morning sun beam shot through the cabin window, warming my face. I looked over at Mr. Lucas' chair which was now empty. The cabin was eerily quiet and I wondered if he was in the cockpit. The sound of a toilet flushing answered that question for me and he soon emerged from the bathroom.

"Well good morning sleepy head," he smiled down at me. "If you have to go potty, go now. We'll be landing in 20 minutes."

I laughed inwardly at his use of the word potty. "Yes Sir," I answered. I actually did need to go. I took my small overnight bag inside the tiny bathroom and tried to freshen up for landing. I used my bottle of water to brush my teeth and wiped my smeared eyeliner from underneath my eyes. My spiral curls were a frizzy mess, so I added a little kiwi oil to tame them, then threw on a little deodorant. There, that definitely made me feel better. When I was finished, I quickly jumped back into my seat belt just in time as we began bumping into some turbulence on our descent.

"Mr. Lucas, are you escorting me all the way?" I asked.

"All the way," he assured me. "I'm not just going to dump you at the airport Claire," he laughed.

I smiled in relief knowing he would stay with me. I don't know what had changed in that short nap I just took, but I woke up with a nervous lump in my tummy. I was feeling very uneasy and had a bad feeling.

Outside my window farm fields rolled beneath, leading a flat path to Houston. I wondered how long it would be until I would see outside of the compound again. How long did they plan on hiding me away here? I secretly took solace in knowing I had the power to fly away from it all if I so desired, but at the same time I would never want to disrespect my commanding officers, especially Chief Master Sergeant Bryant. He was the commanding officer at this facility and had always been so kind to me.

The jet landed softly on the furthest runway out and as soon as the seatbelt light switched off, Lucas stood up and began grabbing our bags.

"Let's go Claire," he commanded. "We have to move quickly here."

I grabbed my things and immediately followed him to the door. He opened it and popped the stairs down, then banged on the cockpit door.

"Thanks fellas!" he yelled above the engines. We scurried down the steps and not far down the runway I could hear the familiar chopping sound of a Blackhawk. A small black van with the door open awaited us. The driver, a short Hispanic man dressed in the same black suit as Mr. Lucas, stood outside the door greeting us with a half smile.

"Credentials please," Mr. Lucas said sternly.

The driver sighed. "Really Lucas?" he asked.

"You know the drill Andreas," Mr. Lucas replied, unapologetically.

I watched as Andreas rolled his eyes, then stared me down curiously as he pulled his wallet from his back pocket, flashing it at Mr. Lucas. I inconspicuously tried to see what kind of badge or card he had, in hopes of knowing the agency they worked for, but he was way too fast for me.

"Everything here secure?" Mr. Lucas said, as we got in the van.

Andreas started the van and the doors locked automatically. "Yes Sir. Ground is secure and both pilots were sent directly from the compound."

"But you still checked their IDs, right?" Lucas asked.

"I did, Sir."

Andreas drove us down the runway and around the backside of a large hanger, where a sleek Blackhawk awaited our arrival. We again quickly grabbed our bags and jumped out of the van.

"Lucas, I'll wait here for you then?" Andreas yelled above the noise.

"Yeah, give me a couple of hours. We'll be on that same bird back."

Lucas and I boarded the chopper and strapped in quickly, throwing our bags behind us and our headphones on. I watched with curiosity as Andreas drove away from the chopper and back towards the plane.

"Mr. Lucas?" I asked through the earphone mic. "Where are you and Andreas going after this?" (I was pretty sure he wouldn't answer, but it was worth a try.)

"My office," he smiled.

"Where's that?" I tried again. He took his finger and drew in the shape of a diamond. It took a moment for it to register. "The Pentagon?" I mouthed quietly.

He nodded his head smiling.

"Maybe I can come visit you there sometime," I suggested.

"Well, our headquarters are there, but it's not an easy find."

"What do you mean?"

"Goodness kid. You are full of nosey questions," he laughed. "How about this; I promise someday I'll take you there. Capisce?"

"Capisce," I smiled reluctantly, then sat back in my seat. Johnny had called me nosey before. Were they right? Was I really that nosey?

ELEVEN

I LOOKED DOWN from the chopper as familiar landscapes began to pop into view; the paved highway that broke off into a two lane winding road, the crystal blue lake, and at last the large shuttle that shined bright and shimmery against the clear blue sky. I sighed at the fate I had earned for myself. How did I land here again and why was it so hard for me to stay out of trouble? Even when I try to do right I do wrong.

I looked over at Lucas who was busy checking out the landscape himself. Who knew when I would see him again? I was really going to miss him. He was like family now.

The Blackhawk now hovered over the red landing circle and slowly began descending. I looked down anxiously wondering where Chief Master Sergeant Bryant was. I had never touched down here when he wasn't waiting for me, holding down his beret in the chopper wind and smiling up, awaiting my arrival.

"Where's CMS Bryant?" I turned around and asked Lucas into my headphone mic. He simply shrugged an "*I don't know"* to my question.

Ten minutes later, we headed toward the ten story high, silver and white, pristine building, toting my luggage behind us. I didn't have much and marveled that all my worldly possessions could fit into two duffles and a backpack. All the Walmart items I had bought in Hawaii were left in my hasty departure. I was sure Sgt. Mancuso was enjoying my hammock, basketball, and all the food left in my apartment fridge.

We walked through the glass doors that led into the two story, bright and glossy foyer. I looked at the hotel-like reception desk that stretched across the foyer and smiled when I saw Jenkins, a pretty redhead, waiting for me in her usual spot. Finally, something familiar.

"Hi Haley," she smiled. I noticed the side glance she gave me, that immediately let me know she had seen the video of me flying.

"Hey Jenkins," I smiled cautiously, unsure of what to say.

"CMS Bryant said to make sure you get your usual room," she smirked as she handed me the room key.

"Thank you. It's my favorite."

We glanced awkwardly at each other for a moment, as I twisted the bottom of my shirt nervously, like I always did under pressure.

"Sooo...what brings you back to our neck of the woods?" she asked at last.

"Haley!" I heard CMS Bryant's familiar voice echo through the lobby. I turned quickly away from Jenkins, all too anxious to leave that conversation.

Jenkins and I stood as straight as we could at attention, until CMS Bryant put us at ease, gave me a quick pat on the shoulder, then walked over to make his introduction to Mr. Lucas. I stayed turned toward them, purposely avoiding Jenkins, but I could feel her stare boring into my back.

"So you got her from here?" I heard Lucas ask.

"Yes we do," CMS Bryant said with confidence.

Mr. Lucas motioned me over and I walked to him while CMS Bryant went to talk to Jenkins.

"Claire, you still got my number?"

"I do."

"You know I'm available to you day or night, right?"

"Yes Sir," I smiled.

"Ok," he smiled back at me, reaching out for our usual fist bump. "I'll be back for you soon, I'm sure."

This was so lame. Do you ever have something happen that triggers a long ago forgotten memory? For some reason my mind went back to my first day of fourth grade when mom was dropping me off at Mrs. Jones' class. (It would have been fine except Mrs. Jones had pale skin and long black hair and my older sister and her friends had told me she was secretly a witch. I was terrified and had this sickening feeling in my stomach after I watched mom walk out of the room, leaving me to fend for myself. In the end, Mrs. Jones actually became one of my favorite teachers of all time, so I learned you can never judge a person by their cover.) Anyway, I know that's a weird comparison, but the emptiness I felt was still the same. I watched as Mr. Lucas disappeared from view, my last glimpse of freedom for a while.

At least CMS Bryant was still here though. He had a way of making me feel at home and like everything was going to be ok.

"Jacobson!" CMS Bryant yelled from behind me. "Give me a hand with Haley's bags!"

"Of course!" I heard a deep voice reply.

My eyes followed the voice down the hall, where my good buddy Jason Jacobson was walking quickly towards us. He was hard to miss with his 6'4" frame, bright blonde hair and blue eyes and today he looked extra tall in his crisp camouflage uniform. Jason had been a former football star in high school and had at one point played overseas professionally, before deciding on a career in the military.

"Claire!" He smiled at me. "Long time no see!"

"Hi Jacobson!" I smiled back, as he gave me a big bear hug.

"Ok, Ok. enough of this," CMS Bryant laughed. "Jacobson, get Haley up to her room."

"That's all you got?" Jason laughed as he grabbed my two duffles.

"Yep," I shrugged, almost ashamed.

CMS Bryant headed down the hall barking orders at me all the way. "Ok Haley, you get settled in today and rest. You'll need to report to Dr. York at 07:00 for a quick check up, then I'll see you in my office at 08:00 sharp."

"Yes Sir," I said, picking up my backpack. I was so grateful to have the rest of the day before all the craziness began.

"I knew you wouldn't last a year," Jacobson teased as we got off the elevator onto the tenth floor.

"What do you mean?" I laughed.

"I knew you couldn't stay out of the sky and it would just be a matter of time before everyone knew."

"Oh," I said, as we stopped in front of my door and I slid the key in. A familiar uneasiness crept into my heart as I remembered the last time I had been at this door with Jacobson. He had all but made a move on me, which I had shut down immediately. No one I had met could even compare to or ever replace Johnny in my heart. If I didn't have him, I didn't want to be with anyone. Oh well, Jason had seemed to move past it now and didn't even seem to remember. Besides, he was one of my poker buddies, as well as a workout buddy, a good listener and friend, so I wanted to just forget it ever happened. "So how did you find out about the rescue?" I asked as we walked into my room.

"Seriously Claire?" he exclaimed, throwing both of my duffles on the bed. "I'm pretty sure the whole world knows now. You're all over social media and the news. The guys here knew immediately it was you."

"They all know?" I asked in shock. Jason just sighed and looked at me, somewhat annoyed that I had even asked. "It's not like I did it on purpose Jason," I defended myself. "I had no choice."

"I'm not blaming you Claire," he laughed.

"CMS Bryant seems like he's ok," I said. "Like he's not mad at me."

"Well, you're the teacher's pet around here," he teased. "You can do no wrong in that man's mind."

"Whatever," I smiled, rolling my eyes at him.

"Well, you get rested up and I'll see you in a bit at lunch."

"Jason, can we make that dinner? I'm not very hungry and I think I might take a nap. That plane ride was a little crazy."

"Yeah sure," Jason said as he headed towards the door. "Six-thirty Claire. Don't be late."

I laid down and melted into the plush bed not realizing how tired I was. I fell fast asleep and didn't wake up until the sun cast a warm evening glow through the curtains.

"Come on Claire! One more!" Jason encouraged me that night in the gym, as I was lying on the bench struggling to get the weights back on the bar above my head. At last I pushed with all my might, extending my arms as the weights clanged loudly back into place.

"Wow girl!" Jason laughed. "What have you been doing the past eight months? I didn't know you were that strong."

"A lot of lifting. Remember I told you I trained with the 180th unit? They are pretty much a top of the line company and their PT kicked my butt."

"Well... excuse me," Jason laughed, rolling his eyes. "Guess they weren't strong enough to keep you grounded though."

I smirked at him. "No one can keep me grounded."

"Well," he said, cocking his head sideways at me. "I think CMS Bryant has every intention to. We discussed it in the briefing."

"Briefing?"

"Yeah. This morning before you arrived."

"Well...what did he say?" I asked, my brow creased with worry.

"Just pretty much that we have to keep you hidden and out of the sky. I have a feeling we'll be doing a lot of dome flying, if any at all."

I sighed in frustration as the double gym doors flew open. Jason turned his eyes toward the door where a group of guys were walking into the gym. I followed his gaze to the men who had their attention focused solely on whoever was walking in the center of them, all laughing at what that person had said. That piqued my curiosity and I did a side glance watching them as inconspicuous as possible. They finally stopped at the treadmill section and a cute little brunette popped up onto the treadmill closest to the mirrors. The guys swarmed around her and as she smiled and cracked another joke, they laughed even louder trying to catch her eye.

This time I was the one rolling my eyes. "*Oh brother,*" I smirked to myself.

I looked over at Jason who was smiling inwardly staring at the girl, but quickly snapped out of it when he noticed my pathetic glare.

"I don't know who she is," he said looking back at me.

I smiled at him. "I didn't ask."

"Oh. Sorry," he laughed, bashfully.

"It's ok," I giggled. "I better get to bed. I have an early day tomorrow."

"Ok," he said, sneaking another look her way. "You want me to walk you up?"

"No thanks. I'm good. See you tomorrow, Jason."

I grabbed my bag and headed for the doors. Several of the guys waved and awkwardly said hello to me, while the others silently whispered amongst themselves, staring wide-eyed in my direction. The girl looked my way and glared curiously and I looked quickly away. She looked so familiar. I knew I had seen her before, but I couldn't put my finger on the when or where.

I was glad to get back to the quietness of my room. I took a long shower and then tried to fall asleep. It wasn't easy. I had grown accustomed to the sound of waves crashing on the shore not far from my little balcony in Hawaii, that had sung me to sleep every night. Sometimes I had even left the door open, just to hear it louder and smell the sweet Hawiian breeze. It was so quiet here. Too quiet. No wind, no jets, no guys talking in the hall. Nothing except emptiness, which matched the mood in my heart.

TWELVE

THE NEXT MORNING I quickly caught the elevator down to the second floor for my appointment with Dr. York. He had been evaluating me for the last two years since I had my accident and probably knew the most about me as far as my body reacting to the mysterious pink potion and how it gave me my flying power.

I stepped off the elevator and headed down the hall towards my usual exam room.

"Airman Haley?" The receptionist called from behind her desk.

"Yes?"

"Dr. York would like for you to wait in the waiting room. He's not quite ready for you yet."

"Oh," I said, a little surprised. "Ok."

I walked into the small waiting room. This was a first.

I had always been instructed to go straight to the exam room and to talk to no one. I waited for a good five minutes until I heard his office door open. Dr. York came out and was talking quietly to someone in the hallway. I couldn't see who it was, only the blurry figure of him and a shorter Airman in the cloudy glass wall they stood behind.

"Ok Dr. York," I heard a female voice softly. "I'll see you in a bit."

I watched the glass curiously as the figure passed the door and headed down the hall. In the small glimpse I got, I could tell it was the same girl that I had seen last night at the gym.

"Airman Haley, you ready?" Dr. York smiled at me as he peeked around the glass.

"Yes Sir," I said and followed him into the exam room. Very soon after a nurse came in to draw my blood. She was a new nurse so I watched her curiously. It was always interesting to see how they would respond when my pink blood would fill the tube, instead of the normal dark red. She popped the needle in my vein, then looked away for a moment. I took a deep breath waiting for her to look back. She grabbed some goss and then checked the needle, looking away and then the double take I had been waiting for. Her eyes grew big and she slightly gasped at the sight of it. I tried to keep a straight face, but it was hard not to laugh. I don't blame her at all. My blood was a weird bright Pepto Bismol pink.

"Dr. York," she said, her eyes frowning in disbelief.

"Ummm.."

Dr. York turned slightly away from his clipboard full of paperwork he was working on and glared at her over his glasses.

"The bl...her blood.." she stammered, pointing at my arm.

"We're all good," he said calmly, turning back to his paperwork. "Just go ahead and close it down. One vial is all we need."

"Ok," she said, looking at me in bewilderment.

All I could offer her was a slight shrug of my shoulders as if I had no idea what was happening.

The nurse quickly gathered her things and left the room after putting the vial on the counter by Dr. York. I kind of felt bad for her, but didn't Jason say everyone here pretty much knew about me now?

"Ok Haley," Dr. York said, picking up the vial. "It looks like everything here is pretty normal looking." He placed a digital thermometer against my head that beeped quickly after. "So, your blood pressure I'll get later when we're in the dome."

"I'm going to the dome today?"

"As far as I know."

Dr. York did his usual routine, checking my eyes and ears, listening to my heart and lungs as I took deep breaths.

"Dr. York?" I asked when he pulled the stethoscope out of his ears. "That girl that you were talking to. Do I know her? She looks very familiar to me."

"I don't think so, Haley. At least I don't know how you could. She's only been here a few weeks."

"Well, what's her name?"

"It's Clarence...umm...Annessa Clarence. She's from Houston."

"What's she doing here?"

Dr. York paused for a moment, then looked at me thoughtfully. "Claire, I'm going to let you discuss that with CMS Bryant. Maybe you can ask him at the meeting this morning."

"Oh...yes Sir," I replied, taking the hint to not press him any further. Dr. York had been so kind to me and I had no desire to put him in an awkward position.

"Alright, you're good to go. You better head downstairs to the conference room. Your meeting starts in about 15 minutes."

"Yes Sir," I said, hopping off the table. "Will you be there?"

"Not this morning, but I'll see ya later at the dome."

"Ok, cool. Thanks Dr. York," I smiled.

I walked quickly to the elevator, hoping to dive into the cafeteria really quick and grab a banana. I had not been hungry before, but felt my tummy suddenly growl.

Downstairs I zipped down the hall and around the corner to the cafeteria and to my surprise came face to face with two men, almost knocking coffee out of the hands of one of them.

"Oh my goodness, please excuse..." I paused looking up at them. Flashes of the meeting in Hawaii popped into my mind. They were both in the same all black uniform and beret I had seen that day. I looked closer at the patch on the beret, surprised to see small pink Saturn rings that looked a lot like mine. I unknowingly glanced down at my tat just to make sure they matched and they did. They were identical.

"Are you ok?" One of the men asked, looking down at my wrist. I quickly tucked it back under the sleeve of my new blue flight suit.

"Oh...yeah," I stammered. "I should watch where I'm going. I'm so sorry."

"You're fine," the other one winked with a smile.

"Well...excuse me please." I gulped and turned to walk to the cafeteria, but not before seeing them chuckle under their breath.

Inside the cafeteria, I waited patiently in line. I had so many questions, though not surprised that this mysterious group seemed to be based from here. Then it hit me all at once. I remembered now. That girl..she was the one at the meeting in Hawaii. Who were they and why did they have my tat on their uniform patches? Now I couldn't wait to get upstairs. I had so many questions for CMS Bryant and I would not leave without answers.

"Haley! Over here!" Jason called from one end of the long conference table he was sitting at.

This room brought back so many memories. My

mom had been with me the first time I ever came here. I remembered being so nervous as I sat between Major Silva and my mom. I would do anything to be with them both right now. I was missing home and my family like crazy and the facetime we had made me miss them even more.

"So do you know what this is all about?" Jason asked as I sat down beside him.

"No," I sighed. "But I'm all meetinged out."

"Oh," Jason laughed. "I can understand that."

"What are you doing here? Are you running security at the dome again?"

Jason sat back in his chair and folded his arms across his chest. "Well, yes and no. I've actually been assisting more in security all over the base. They promoted me about 3 months ago."

My eyes lit up. "Jason! Oh my goodness! I'm so proud of you!"

"Thanks sweetie," he blushed.

"What exactly does that include?"

"Well, I pretty much have access to all areas of the base except the higher ups offices. We have been on level red since we knew you were coming and we've worked day and night to make sure the base is extra secure."

"Oh," I said, biting my lip a little ashamed of all the trouble I caused. "Sooo...you're pretty much meetinged out too?" I asked.

"A little, but I guess you're worth it," he laughed and then looked past me toward the door. I turned to see what he was staring at and of course it was the girl from last night. She was followed by the two guys from downstairs and all were dressed in the same black uniform. She glanced over my way and smiled slightly. I was definitely sure now she was the same girl who was at my meeting in Hawaii. I looked back at Jason, who watched her until she sat a few chairs down the table from us.

"Gosh Jason, drool much?"

"Man Claire, she looks so much like you," Jason said, looking me up and down.

"No she doesn't," I snapped back.

CMS Bryant followed in behind her, making his way to the middle of the conference table. This meeting was small in number, with only Jason and I, Commander Whitley, (who was a former astronaut and in charge of all procedures in the dome) and then the three of them.

CMS Bryant cleared his throat and then sat across from all of us. "Ok...where do I begin," he said mainly to himself, then looked my way. "Well, first I want to welcome Airman Haley back. I know the circumstances for you being with us aren't ideal and you'd rather be back in Hawaii, but at least here you are safe. We hope that we can make greater progress in figuring out what is going on with you and this whole situation."

I nodded and smiled at him, but boy was he right about the wanting to be back in Hawaii, part.

"So I'm just going to introduce everyone here and then we'll get into what everyone's role is, while Haley is with us." He nodded down the table toward Jason. "This is Staff Sergeant Jacobson, he is in charge of security while

Haley is here, specifically in the dome." Jason awkwardly smiled and waved at everyone. What a goof.

CMS Bryant then nodded to Whitley, who sat beside me. "Commander Whitley is on loan to us again from NASA, he will be assisting in the dome with flying."

And now the part I had been waiting for-the three Amigos all dressed in black.

"I'd like for you all to meet Astronaut Candidate Clarence, who will be working with us the next few weeks and with her is her support team, Officer Brady and Officer Grant."

I looked down the table at them. Did he say Astronaut Candidate? I glanced at Jason who looked as shocked as I did and mouthed "*Astronaut Candidate?*" to me.

CMS Bryant continued for the next several minutes going over security, schedules and what my limitations would be as far as flying.

"Just so you know, this base is under strict radar control. No one can get on or off without our knowledge, whether they walk through the front gate or fly in by helicopter." CMS Bryant didn't look directly at me, but I was pretty sure he was subtly hinting that I could not fly outside and there was no way I could escape undetected.

"Airman Haley and AC Clarence, I'm going to give you both an hour to maybe just go get some coffee and get acquainted before we meet back in the dome at 10. Please be in your flight gear."

"Yes Sir," I heard myself say in unison with her.

We were dismissed and I stood up beside Jason.

"Well Claire, I'll see you in a bit," he said. "I have to go do my rounds before dome time."

"Ok, see you soon," I said, watching him leave. I was a bit confused. Why was I being asked to hang out with this girl and get to know her? Don't get me wrong, I love to meet new people and make new friends and I was definitely excited about having another girl around, but I felt like we were being forced together for some weird reason. I wondered if she was feeling that too.

I watched the men leave the room in twos following Jason. First CMS Bryant with Commander Whitley, then the two Officers. I turned and looked at AC Clarence who was looking back at me.

"Hi," I said, walking over to her. "I'm Claire."

"I know," she smiled. "My name is Annessa."

"Nice to meet you." She had a kind smile and seemed genuinely nice.

We walked down to the cafe and began our somewhat awkward conversation of figuring each other out. Me, being the impatient person I was, got right to the point.

"So why are you here if you're training to be an astronaut?" I asked, as we sipped our lattes in the quiet coffee shop.

Annessa cocked her head sideways, almost pausing thoughtfully, "Well, I think they thought learning from and being around you would help my training."

"They who?" I asked. "Who do you work for and why is my tat on your uniform patch?"

Annessa's eyebrows shot up, surprised by my questions.

I didn't mean to sound as confrontational as I did, but my curiosity got the best of me. "I work for NASA and I have no idea what you're talking about," she said pointedly.

I put my left arm on the table and she leaned over to examine it closely, then took off her beret to compare the two. "I have no idea," she repeated, her eyes blinking as if she didn't believe what she was seeing. "Honestly, this is just the unit they assigned me to and well... I didn't design the uniforms."

I stared down at the beret and my wrist. It made no sense. "So they didn't tell you at all why you're here?"

"They said research and observation."

"Oh," I said, not fully convinced. "You mean like as far as gravity goes?"

"Yeah," she said, almost relieved that I had offered an answer to my own question. "They were going to send me to Hawaii to work with you there, but then everything happened. I hope you're ok with me hanging out and watching."

I smiled, trying to smooth over my abrasiveness. "Of course. The whole world pretty much knows now anyway."

"Claire, do you mind telling me your story and what happened to you?"

I paused for a moment. "Well, do you mind if we start with you first? I usually do all the storytelling and I'm definitely curious as to how you became an astronaut at such a young age. I mean, how old are you?"

"Twenty-four."

I gasped at her reply. Only 5 years older than me.

How could someone so young already be in an advanced astronaut program? Those positions usually took a whole career to achieve.

"I graduated high school at fifteen," she said, as if reading my mind.

So Annessa Clarence had quite a story and she immediately drew me into it. She never knew her dad and when she was just 4 years old, her mom who had a horrible drug addiction problem, dropped her off at her grandma's house on a cold, wintery Christmas Eve night. She had promised she would return before the holiday for Annessa, but was never heard from again.

"...so I don't even know if she's dead or alive," she sighed, nonchalantly.

"I'm so sorry," I said as we walked toward the dome.

Annessa shrugged it off. "It was so long ago, so I barely remember her. But anyway, my grandmother died when I was 8 and after that, I got bounced around from foster home to foster home. My fascination with flight and the deep mystery of space is what saved me and why I worked so hard to get where I am."

"I definitely can relate...to the flying part," I agreed.

Annessa paused on the sidewalk as we approached the dome. "When I saw you flying in that video Claire, I thought to myself how incredibly lucky you are." She looked up at the perfectly clear sky. "You can fly anytime you want. No planes, no parachutes, or rockets. Just you and the open sky. I can't imagine having that."

I nodded in agreement. I was very blessed and there

wasn't a day that passed, that I didn't thank God for my gift.

"I feel very fortunate," I said. "But there's a scary side too. My body worries me a bit. I mean, *I have pink blood* and I have *no* idea how it will affect me long term." We started our walk to the dome again. "I used to let it worry me a lot, but now I just go with the flow. I don't want to live the rest of my life in fear."

"I agree," Annessa smiled. "Sometimes you just have to take chances."

THIRTEEN

TWENTY MINUTES LATER I stood in the center of the dome, all suited up with monitors stuck to me to keep my heart rate intact. Annessa stared up at me, her eyes wide as Commander Whitley made a few adjustments on the monitors and his laptop.

"Why so many CAM tabs?" she asked. I raised my eyebrows at her, not having a clue as to what she was talking about. "The patches on you," she explained.

Dr. York looked curiously at the laptop screen. "Because of her blood type," he answered, not looking in our direction.

"See?" I whispered to Annessa. "It's the not knowing, that's the hard part."

Annessa smiled sympathetically at me.

"Jacobson, are we good to go on the perimeter?" CMS

Bryant asked.

"Yes Sir!" Jason called from the door, giving two thumbs up.

At last it was time to fly. My chest tightened and my tat glowed a bright pink. I felt gravity leave my body, as I quickly lifted off the ground then held at my usual 50 feet in the air, until given permission to go higher. Annessa looked up at me, her blue eyes wide in wonder. Maybe Jason was right. She did resemble me a little.

"Ok Claire, let's go!" Commander Whitley ordered.

I shot straight into the air thankful that at least I could get off the ground, despite being trapped inside. I went through the familiar drills as instructed and each time I touched down, Annessa would approach me, checking out my tat and asking us all kinds of questions. She paid extra attention to every word Commander Whitley said, even writing things down on her little notepad. Before I knew it three hours had passed.

"Ok Haley, I want you and Clarence back here tomorrow at 08:00 hours," CMS Bryant stated. "We're going to start a little earlier."

Annessa and I were dismissed and then left the dome for the cafeteria. It was well after one and neither of us had lunch yet.

"Hey Claire, want to hang out after dinner tonight?" she asked.

"Of course," I smiled. "I need some girl time. I've been around guys non-stop."

"Oh, me too," she laughed. "They say girls are gossipy

and chatty, but I've learned otherwise."

"Yes!" I agreed. "And talk about cliquish! It's harder to break into their friendship circles than Area 51." She shot an inquisitive glance at me. "Not that I've ever tried, Miss Astronaut USA."

We both laughed and headed into the cafeteria for lunch. Maybe my stay here wouldn't be so bad. I was excited for my blooming new friendship with Annessa.

That night I returned to my room exhausted, having spent all evening at the base pool with Annessa, Jason, and a few of the guys. Jason had walked Annessa back to her room on the floor just below mine and I was A-ok with that. I liked Jason, but felt relieved that his personal interest in me had now shifted to her. It made everything much less complicated.

George Strait played through my bluetooth as I jumped in the shower. I was feeling a little homesick and his music always took me back to Tennessee. "*Amarillo By Morning*" was about halfway through when my phone rang. It was probably my mom and I would call her as soon as I got out, but I was still washing the conditioner out of my hair when it rang again.

I grabbed a towel and threw it on my hair, then wrapped another one around me and jumped out to answer.

"Hello?" I said out of breath on the final ring.

"Claire?"

I gasped as Johnny's deep voice filled my world again. It had been so long since I had talked to him and I struggled to even get one word out.

"Claire, it's Johnny," he tried again. "Can you hear me?"

"Johnny," I repeated, not knowing what else to say. All kinds of emotions filled my heart and mind and I didn't know whether to be bitter because I hadn't heard from him in so long or relieved that I finally was.

"Yeah...are you ok?"

I bit my lip in frustration. "Am I ok? I haven't...I haven't heard from you in over 2 months Johnny. Not a call or a text or an email...or...or even a message from Silva. How could you just leave me hanging like that?"

Johnny spoke quickly. "I know Claire...I know. I'm so sorry. I know you're not going to believe this, but my phone fell out of my pocket during flight, on a mission over the desert and... and it didn't matter anyway, because I had no service most of the time there."

I was quiet for a moment. I still didn't understand how he had no possible way to reach me.

"Another thing," he said hesitantly, "I was in the hospital for about a month..."

I gasped. "What? Oh my gosh, are you ok?"

"Yeah, my head just got a little rattled during an emergency landing in a Hawk."

I paused in disbelief. I felt like a jerk. "What did the doctor say?" I asked slowly, fearing what his answer would be. A thousand bad thoughts ran through my mind. The brain is such a fragile miracle and extremely vulnerable at the same time. I couldn't imagine something ever happening to my Johnny or even him having to give up his dream of piloting. He had worked so hard to achieve it.

"The doctor said I'm fine and they will just do regular check ups on me."

I breathed a sigh of relief. "Were you flying it?"

"Not this time. Something went wrong with the tail rotor, so there was nothing the pilot could do. We still don't know what caused it."

Typical Johnny to never blame someone else or find anything negative to say about another soldier. That pilot could have been 100% at fault and he still wouldn't have told me.

"How could no one have told me this? Did Silva know?" I asked, sitting down on the end of my bed.

"Yeah, I just...I didn't think it was a good idea for him to tell you. You were struggling through training there and I didn't want you stressing about me on top of it all."

"Johnny," I said, trying not to sound irritated with him. "Of course, I'd wanna know about that. If it was me, wouldn't you?"

"Well, yeah.."

"Besides, I thought we promised no more secrets ever, right?"

He sighed. "We did...Claire, I miss you so much." I winced at the desperation and sadness in his voice.

"I miss you too," I whispered, my heart aching. " You have no idea how much." All the feelings of loneliness and sadness over Johnny, I had worked so hard to push away from these past few months, came flooding back in a hurry. My eyes filled with tears and I tried desperately not to cry over the phone. I didn't want him to have anything more to worry about.

"Claire, I know you. You're trying not to cry...and you're doing a horrible job as usual," he laughed softly.

"I'm so sorry," I smiled through my tears. He knew me so well.

"Claire Bear, I made up my mind. I'm not ever going to be away from you again. I don't know what I need to do to make that happen, but I refuse to be separated from you anymore."

I smiled at his sweetness. "I agree," I sniffled. "I never want to leave you again."

"Well then it's settled. You're getting stuck with me and that's that."

"Poor guy," I sniffled again.

"So I guess you're too famous to want to stay with a regular Joe like me now, huh?"

"What?"

"The flying thing?"

"Oh, you saw that?" I gasped.

"Well, who hasn't?" he chuckled. "Good grief Claire, what were you thinking?"

"I had to Johnny..."

"Yeah, ok," he laughed again. "Whatever made these guys think they could keep you out of the air is beyond me."

I laughed with him. He always made me feel better despite how down I was. "You know I get it from you right?"

"I guess that's why we're so perfect together."

"Yeppers," I whispered.

"Claire, I'm going to try and get home by Christmas, but in the meantime, I'm going to ask for a four day to come see you."

"When?"

"Soon," he promised.

We talked a few more minutes about him coming and my heart beat with so much excitement at the thought of seeing him again.

"Johnny, I love you," I said as we hung up.

"I love you too, my Claire Bear. Sweet dreams and I'll be seeing you soon."

The next two weeks seemed to fly by as Annessa and I busied ourselves in the dome and hanging out. I thought for sure she would be spending more time with Jason than me, but for some reason the opposite was true and I didn't mind at all. I really liked Annessa and was glad I had someone here to hang out with. We had everything in common from working out to our love of 80's music. In Hawaii I had Zhao and he was such a blast, but having a girl was a different ballgame. She was a little older than me, but was so enthralled with my ability to fly and made me feel like some kind of a celebrity, always following me around. And the questions! Oh my goodness! She was always asking questions.

On a stormy Thursday night, we sat on my bed, her on her laptop and me on mine, shopping for clothes and listening to the Jets, "Crush on You" stream from my bluetooth. With no clothing stores around, this was the only way we could shop and since I had left Hawaii with practically nothing, I needed more clothes and stuff. We didn't mind though. We would order at the same time, then wait for both of our packages to come in and do a fashion show for each other. Sometimes the clothes were spot on and sometimes we were way off. You never knew what you would get shopping online. When they were terrible, we would laugh uncontrollably at how awful we looked. Sometimes that laughfest was worth all the trouble of having to send them back.

On this night in particular, I was shopping for a simple and comfortable black dress I could wear while Johnny was here. Nothing fancy, just light and summery.

"How 'bout this one, Claire?" She asked, turning her laptop towards me. "See the cute little eyelet sleeve?"

"Oh that is so cute Nessa," I said, pulling up a closer image.

"When is Johnny coming?" she asked.

"Umm...he's thinking by Thanksgiving."

"That's only 2 weeks!" she exclaimed.

"I know!" I said, clapping my hands softly. "I can't wait to see him."

"You're so lucky," she smiled, though her eyes looked sad.

"What do you mean?"

"You have a great boyfriend, a great family...you can fly..."

"Annessa, Jason likes you," I teased.

Annessa just smiled and shrugged at me.

"You don't like Jason?"

"I like him," she shrugged again, "But I don't know, there's just something different about him. Something I just can't put my finger on."

I nodded in agreement with her. There was something different, but I just took it as him having no game with girls. Whatever it was, it was enough to keep both of us away.

"Well Annessa, you're a part of my family now."

She smirked at me like I was joking.

"No seriously," I said. "You should come home with me for Christmas this year. I know my mom wouldn't mind and my family would love you."

"Seriously?"

"Yes! You will love my family and my town. Tennessee is such a beautiful place."

She was just about to answer, when my messenger Facetime went off. To my utter surprise it was my best friend Alicia.

"Mony!" I screamed before she could even say hello.

"Clairey!" She screamed back.

"Omgoodness! What are you doing?"

"I'm sending you a pic," she beamed holding up her phone. "I want to see your face when you open it."

My text immediately dinged and I opened the pic. It was Alicia, standing on a platform in a beautiful, white wedding gown. I recognized it immediately as my top choice from the couple of dozen she had sent to me over the past three months. The slim fitting dress curved her perfectly then slowly flared out at the bottom. I loved the see through straps laced with a white, viney flower that flowed all the way down her back. It was very whimsical and fairy-like and her dark hispanic skin made the white pop even more.

"Oh Mony, it's so beautiful," I said, not taking my eyes off the picture. "You're so beautiful. It's just perfect."

"Well, you helped me. I probably would have never given this one a second thought, but I'm just so in love with it now."

"Aww," I smiled. "You look beautiful in anything. Can I show it to Annessa?"

"Of course!"

Annessa slid beside me and gasped. "It's so beautiful!"

"Thanks!" Alicia said.

"Oh!" I said, remembering my manners. "Annessa, this is my best friend Alicia, aka Mony."

"Mony?" Annessa laughed.

"Her nickname for me since forever," Alicia cringed. "Something to do with the Mona Lisa...Mona Alicia?"

"I was five when I started calling you that," I defended myself, laughing. "Besides, I think it's cute."

Alicia shook her head, smiling. "Anyway, it's so nice to meet you, Annessa. Claire has told me so many great things about you."

Annessa smiled, "Same here. I can tell she really misses you. All of you guys."

"Did you and Shawn figure out a date for the wedding?" I asked.

"Yes!" Alicia said, leaning into the camera like it was some kind of secret. "What do you think about Valentine's Day? It's on a Saturday, plus Shawn said it will help him remember our anniversary every year."

Annessa and I both laughed. "You don't have to get my approval, Mony. Just let me know and I'll be there."

"Well, I just want to make sure it won't interfere with everything that's going on with you, Clairey. I won't get married unless you are there, you know."

"Aww," I said, reaching down and touching the screen. "Nothing would ever keep me away from your wedding. I will fly myself there if I have to."

Annessa and I spent the next twenty minutes talking to Alicia as we made final plans for her wedding.

"You know you're invited too, Annessa," Alicia said as we were hanging up.

"Oh wow, thank you," Annessa gushed, then looked at me after we hung up. "She's so nice Claire."

"Yeah, she's pretty great," I agreed.

Annessa folded up her laptop and tucked it into the case. "Well, I better get to bed. I guess we have a busy day tomorrow."

"I know. Any clue as to where they are taking us?" I yawned, following her to the door.

"I was going to ask you the same thing," she laughed. "I don't have a clue."

"Commander Whitley seemed pretty excited about it," I shrugged. "At least it gets us past the gates of the base for a while."

"Definitely," she agreed. "Well, I'll see you in the morning at 08:00 Supergirl."

"Good night Annessa," I smiled.

FOURTEEN

THE NEXT MORNING we were in an unmarked van, heading off the base with Commander Whitley, CMS Bryant, one driver (who appeared to be a lowly ranking member like myself) and two armed guards in a jeep behind us.

I stared at the gates as they opened and the guard waved us through. I wondered how long it would be until I could leave through the gates again for good. Don't get me wrong, I enjoyed all the people I worked with here, but I wanted to go back to Campbell where my family, friends and Johnny were, especially now that Johnny was stateside again.

"Is that Jason behind us?" I asked Annessa as I glanced out the back window from the last seat in the back of the van. It was too hard to tell with the tinted windows.

"Yes," she smiled and rolled her eyes. "He practically begged CMS Bryant to come."

"Oh," I cringed. "Either he has really bad cabin fever like us or he just looks for every excuse imaginable to be with you."

"Whatever," she laughed.

"It's true Annessa," I teased, "but I'm just so glad to get out for a while. Three weeks stuck in there and I'm about to lose my sanity."

Annessa looked at me sympathetically. "I know you said you hate this Claire, but you'll probably have to get used to it eventually."

"Get used to what?" I asked, squinting my nose at her curiously.

"This. The armed guards, someone constantly watching your back. You're a hot commodity...a much *sought* after commodity."

"Well, that's not happening Annessa," I whispered, sitting back in my seat and crossing my arms, stubbornly. I glanced up to make sure the higher ups couldn't hear me. "I refuse to live the rest of my life hiding behind some gated wall, scared to go anywhere. That's not who I am."

Annessa leaned back beside me. "I would live the rest of my life doing whatever they told me to do, as long as I had your flying power. Aren't you afraid they're going to take it away from you if you don't comply?"

"No," I smirked. "That could never happen."

Annessa glared at me. "How do you know?" she asked. "You said yourself, there's so much to it you don't understand."

"That's true," I agreed, "but there's also a lot of it I do understand and my flying power is not going anywhere. It's like it's infused into my being and who I am...I don't know how to describe it. I just...I just know it will always be."

"Believe it or not, I totally understand that," Annessa smiled. "I still think you're the luckiest girl on this planet."

Forty five minutes later, we turned west on a small two lane road, surrounded on either side by thick, dry brush. Down the road I could see a small forest of trees that seemed out of place in this dry area. The van drove into the canopy tunnel of trees, eventually slowing down at a small gravel road that was blocked by a simple chain strung across two metal poles on either side. A sign that read,

"RESTRICTED AREA, TRESPASSERS WILL BE PUNISHED TO THE HIGHEST EXTENT OF THE LAW. AREA UNDER MILITARY SURVEILLANCE."

"*Great, here we go again,*" I thought to myself. I had seen way too many restricted signs lately.

"Yep, this is it," Commander Whitley said to the driver as we turned on the gravel road. I stole a glance over at Annessa who seemed as confused as I did.

The van rounded the corner and pulled silently to a stop beside another unmarked government vehicle, in front of a simple and small white brick building. (I only knew that it belonged to the government because Johnny had taught me how to read license plates thinking somehow it would keep me safer.)

I slid out of the van and looked around, listening to the trees rustling in the morning wind. Birds were singing and the sweet smell of fresh cut grass filled my senses. This place almost reminded me of home.

"Claire!" Jason said, interrupting my thoughts. He was standing with the door open to the building, waving me inside. Everyone else must have already gone in, because I was the only one out, except for Jason who refused to leave me alone.

"Oh! Sorry Jay," I smiled, following him inside. Once inside, I immediately noticed the pristine white walls, ceiling and floor. A shiny black counter stood out in the middle of the room in contrast to the brightness around it.

"Claire!" I heard a familiar voice say. I turned around, not sure if I was hearing right.

My eyes squinted as I scanned the room in search of his face. At last I saw his bright smile, popping off his brown skin. "Zhao!" I squealed, as he ran up and bear-hugged me, twirling us around. "Oh my god! What are you doing here?"

"I'm here with my dad and I...I have no idea," he laughed.

"I'm so glad to see you," I smiled as he set me back on

the ground.

"Hello Claire," Dr. Zhao said as he walked over and joined us.

"Hey Dr. Zhao!" I exclaimed, unable to contain my excitement. "What are you guys doing here?" I asked again.

"Well, come here and let's see," he winked at me, nodding toward the black counter.

I linked my arm with my Zhao's, still in total shock he was here, as we joined everyone who had huddled around the counter, including an elderly man who was dressed in a simple white polo and khakis. I glanced toward the door where Jason stood casting curious looks at Zhao, between peeks at the door. The van driver was now pulling double duty as the guard outside.

CMS Bryant cleared his throat. "Alright, let's get to this. Everyone, this is Dr. Zhao, he is one of our top scientists at NASA and this is his protege, Airman Zhao, both of whom worked with Claire in Hawaii. This is his partner Dr. Albert and they have been working together here at Area 27 and Houston under the direction of the late Major Brian Kearney."

My eyes shot open at the mention of Brian Kearney's name. He was the first name I had discovered on my quest to figure out my flying power at the beginning of all this. I noticed Dr. Zhao looked over at me and smiled slightly at my reaction.

Dr. Albert then took the floor. "Claire, it's a pleasure to finally meet you. I know you have a lot of unanswered questions and I'm hoping to answer some of them today."

I nodded, a little surprised. I had no idea this little field trip had anything to do with my flying research.

Dr. Albert reached into his pocket and pulled out what appeared to be a flashdrive. He plugged it into some kind of an outlet underneath the counter and behind him a small screen automatically slid down from the ceiling. I watched as a picture appeared that seemed to be very old. In it a man stood beside a large hole in the ground that was about six feet deep and roughly the size of a small car. The dirt in the hole and the brush all around was scorched black and the man stood beside it grinning from ear to ear.

"So this is Major John Kearney. He was stationed at Sheppard Air Force base during the war. On October 7th, 1944, an asteroid crashed near here and Major Kearney was sent to investigate and gather rock samples."

"When you say near here do you mean this facility?" Annessa asked, pointing behind her.

"That's right Annessa," he answered. "When Major Kearney arrived he found this big crater in the woods with most of the asteroid disintegrated, however some small pieces remained."

The picture on the next slide made us all catch our breath. Major Kearney knelt beside the hole and a closer look revealed small to medium sized rocks that seemed to be floating out of the hole in the ground.

Zhao gasped, "Are those rocks floating?"

"Yes Sir," Dr. Albert replied. "To his surprise they were basically gravity proof, but still amazingly didn't float off the planet. The Air Force restricted the area and Major Kearney spent the next two months gathering as many as he could. He dissected them and was surprised to find inside…"

"The pink potion…" I whispered aloud.

"That's right Claire," Dr. Zhao said. "He spent years extracting the pink liquid from the rocks that he called "Rocket Juice." When he developed cancer, he passed all the information to his son Ron and then finally to his grandson Brian. All were high ranking members of the Air Force and eventually Brian worked with us."

"But you never knew Brian could fly," I reminded him.

"True," Dr. Zhao agreed, "But we didn't know anything about him making a flying potion. Our focus was on the rocks and how they were unaffected by gravity with the pink liquid inside. We had joked around about it working on humans or animals, but we didn't know Brian was experimenting with that and definitely had no idea he had consumed it."

I sat dumbfounded, shaking my head in disbelief, while every eye seemed to be on me. The room was eerily quiet.

At last Zhao looked at his dad. "So basically, Claire's flying power comes from some other planet and there is no way to know how long she'll have it or how it will affect her long term?"

"Pretty much," Dr. Zhao confirmed, bowing his head. "But we're not giving up."

My body quivered at the thought of that. I didn't even

like taking a Tylenol unless I had to, so having a liquid from another planet inside my body was too overwhelming. My head started to spin and I felt a little queasy.

"Do you know what planet?" Zhao asked. I was so thankful for his questions, because at this point I couldn't think right. Like a true friend, Zhao always had my back and my best interests at heart.

"Not so sure," Dr. Albert said. "We have a pretty good guess, but nothing definite."

"What planet?" Annessa asked, wide-eyed.

"Have you ever heard of Zeta Reticuli?" Dr. Albert asked.

"Of course," Annessa answered. (She is so smart. I had never heard of that.)

"One of those stars," he answered.

"But Claire," Dr. Zhao said, turning to me again. "We will never stop our efforts of trying to figure it all out and we'll continue to work with you, to make sure you have as normal and healthy a life as possible. We just thought you deserve to know the history behind your power."

I smiled at them both and thanked them. I appreciated their help and at least they were trying. "The crash site is around here?" I asked.

"Yes Ma'am," Dr. Albert replied. "We can go if it's ok," he said looking over at CMS Bryant.

"It's fine with me," CMS Bryant nodded over to Jason, who in turn went outside to check the perimeter.

Dr. Albert led us outside. "It's just a two minute walk through the trees."

On the walk there, I introduced Annessa to Zhao and could tell she was absolutely smitten. She asked him all kinds of questions about his background and Zhao was more than happy to oblige.

The trees soon parted and we came to a small cliff that rose beside a flat prairie. A tall, solid white fence surrounded the area and Dr. Albert opened the padlock allowing us inside. The crater appeared much bigger than the original picture and I assumed it had been from years of digging and research. It was still fascinating to see the big hole it caused. It must have been a huge meteorite.

"As you can see, we've pretty much taken all the samples available," Dr. Albert explained.

"Where are the rocks now?" Jason asked from the door of the fence.

"NASA," Dr. Zhao said simply.

"Claire, look at your tat!" Zhao exclaimed, grabbing my arm.

I looked down at my wrist that was now glowing the brightest pink I had ever seen. It was almost fluorescent and had it been night, it would have lit up the whole crater. Annessa was quickly by my side and touching my arm while squinting her eyes from the bright light. Everyone else gathered around and I stood there gawking at it, as entranced as they were. Dr. Zhao took out his phone and began to snap pictures while Zhao videoed.

"That's insane," I heard Jason whisper behind us. "It's like the tat knows its own. Like it has a connection here."

"I feel like some kind of an alien," I complained to Zhao, Annessa and Jason that night at dinner.

Zhao smiled at me sympathetically. "You're not an alien, Claire."

Annessa took a bite of her Caesar salad and then tried to reassure me with her mouth full. "Goodness Claire, do you know how many girls would die to be in your shoes?"

"Yeah and that tat trick was the coolest thing I've seen in a long time," Jason said.

I looked at Zhao who was looking at my tat that had pretty much returned to the normal gray and pink, except for a few bright pink streaks around the Saturn rings that were still glowing. "Why do you think that happened?" I asked.

"I'm not sure Claire," he shrugged. "My dad thinks it might be because of some radioactive residue left from the crash...but that's just a guess. Those rocks were not like anything we have on earth obviously."

"Where are the rocks now?" Jason asked.

"I don't know," Zhao answered. "That's pretty much classified information. I just wish there was more we knew that we could share with you Claire. It's just hard because the crash happened so long ago and all we have to work with are the rock shells and a vial of the rocket juice."

"A vial?" I asked. "Zhao, I think there's more than one. At Campbell there were at least two."

Zhao's eyes grew wide. "Two? Are you sure Claire? I've only heard of one."

"Positive," I reassured him. I glanced over at Annessa, who seemed to grow disinterested in our conversation and was staring down quietly at her half eaten salad. The table grew strangely uncomfortable.

Jason leaned back in his seat and stretched. "Well, you guys better figure that one out soon," he yawned. "You wouldn't want it to end up in the wrong hands."

"I'll ask my dad and see if he knows anything," Zhao reassured me, grabbing my hand. "Don't worry. We'll figure it out."

I smiled back at my friend. I felt so much better having him and Dr. Zhao here.

FIFTEEN

"WHERE'S ANNESSA?" ZHAO asked the next day as we walked towards the dome.

"I don't know," I said, pulling my hair in a bun. "She skipped breakfast this morning, so I'm not sure." I smiled mischievously, "And why are you so interested?"

"Oh please Claire," he laughed, rolling his eyes, then looked up at the towering dome above us. "So this is the famous dome you always spoke of."

"Yep, the most exciting thing on this base," I said dryly.

Zhao nodded his head agreeing with me. "I can certainly see why you didn't want to leave Hawaii."

The wind whipped past us in a roar as we opened the door to the dome. Jason was there to greet us and make sure the bolt was secure as it snapped back into place. I was surprised to see Annessa already there and out on the dome floor with CMS Bryant, Commander Whitley, Dr. York and Dr. Zhao.

Dr. York was checking Annessa's blood pressure through her blue NASA suit and I noticed ropes hanging high from the rafters of the ten story building.

"What's going on?" I said under my breath to Zhao, as we approached them and everyone grew quiet. I looked up at the ropes that seemed to go on forever above us.

"What are you guys doing? I asked, as everyone avoided eye contact with me and looked at Commander Whitley.

I followed their gaze to Commander Whitley who cleared his throat and looked directly at me. "Claire, we're doing some extra testing and have decided to take our research to the next level for your sake. Annessa has generously agreed to help us."

I looked at Annessa who had belay links hooked to a vest that was strapped between her legs and over the shoulders. I was so confused.

"How does pulling Annessa up by ropes help with figuring out how I fly?" I laughed awkwardly.

Everyone grew quiet again as I scanned their eyes for the answer, again stopping at Commander Whitley for an explanation.

"We're not pulling her up," he said cautiously. "She's... we injected her with the rocket juice. She's going to fly."

I gasped, my eyes furrowing in a mixture of shock and anger, but mostly concern. I backed up away from the group, unsure of what to say.

"Well, that explains where the other vial went," Zhao

said to me through clenched teeth.

"Claire it's ok," CMS Bryant tried to assure me.

"No, it's not Sir. Are you guys crazy?" I glanced back and forth at all of them. "Are *you* crazy?" I asked Annessa, looking at her specifically.

"Claire..." she began.

"No!" I shouted. "Do you remember what happened to Brian Kearney? Do you remember at all? Well here's a reminder! He's dead! He dropped out of the sky trying to fly!"

It grew quiet again, then Commander Whitley crossed his arms and spoke quieter in an attempt to calm me down. "That's not going to happen here Claire," he said. "We are taking all the necessary precautions to ensure that it doesn't and Annessa is safe."

"But her body...I mean you still can't even figure out mine." I looked at Dr. York while trying desperately to hold back tears.

Dr. York walked over to me and wrapped his arm around my shoulder. "Claire, we wouldn't do this if we didn't feel it was safe for Annessa. Everything about her mirrors you. Her blood type, height, her physical attributes..."

"Her DNA?" I asked. "Does she have the rings?" I lifted my wrist for all to see. They burned a bright pink in my aggravation.

Dr. York looked at me for a moment and I could tell I had him thinking. "Not yet," he said.

"Well, that might be an important factor considering

it's been a big part of my flying power. With all due respect, this is a mistake, a huge mistake and I'll have no part in it." I turned and ran quickly to the door of the dome.

"Claire, wait…" Jason said, stepping in front of the exit.

"Move Jason," I demanded.

Jason looked down at the ground, reluctantly opening the door as I sailed past him and up to my room. Once I was there, I locked the door and didn't answer it or my phone for the rest of the day.

I fell into a deep sleep that evening and per usual when stressed, had a crazy dream. In my dream I was standing on a podium at what appeared to be an outdoor 60's rock concert. I looked over the vast audience of thousands of fans who were yelling for me to fly. I tried to calm the crowd down, but the more I tried, the more agitated they grew. At last I looked into the audience and from the middle of the crowd halfway back, I saw Annessa in a black, flowing hippie dress slowly rise into the dark sky, thick with storm clouds. Immediately the people turned and began cheering her on. She smiled and waved down at them and then waved at me. In the distance a clap of thunder lit up the sky and she suddenly slipped straight down, disappearing from sight.

A light tapping on the door and a loud clap of lightning woke me from my sleep. I looked at the clock which read

10:45. Who would be bothering me this late at night? I rolled out of bed and stumbled my way to the door, looking out the peephole. Zhao and his dad looked up, their noses big and round in the glass. I slowly removed the chain and unlocked the dead bolt.

"Hey Claire," Zhao smiled stiffly at me. "Mind if we come in?"

I stepped aside and rubbed my eyes. "Not at all," I yawned.

"We brought you dinner," Zhao said, holding up a white styrofoam container. Something warm, onioney and spicy filled the air as he waved the container in front of me. I wondered if it was some kind of authentic cuisine from their native country of Japan. Whatever it was it smelled amazing, making my stomach growl. I had forgotten I hadn't eaten all day.

"Wow, thanks you guys," I said as he placed it in my hands.

"You ok Claire?" Dr. Zhao asked, as we sat in my tiny couch area that consisted of just a loveseat and reading chair.

"Yeah, I'm fine. I just can't believe this."

Zhao sat beside me on the loveseat and put his arm around me. "Well, just so you know, my dad and I had nothing to do with this."

Dr. Zhao cleared his throat. "Well I knew, but I voted against it. I just don't see the benefit of it all."

"Same here," I agreed. "It makes no sense to try and solve something by compounding it."

"Well Claire," said Dr. Zhao. "I can assure you that this is being done with the best intentions. They really think the two of you together might help figure you out and trust me when I say, CMS Bryant has been very vocal about your safety."

I leaned back on the couch crossing my arms in defiance. "Dr. Zhao, that makes no sense. Who creates two disasters to solve one? Besides, this is not safe for Annessa. Just because we have the same hair color, does not mean the rocket juice will react the same in our bodies."

"I know," he sighed, throwing up both hands. "But just give us some slack please. We really are trying to do what's best for you. Maybe this will work, maybe not, but it's worth a try to help you out."

"What about you dad? Are you a maybe or a maybe not?" Zhao asked sincerely.

Dr. Zhao paused for a moment before answering.

"Come on...honest truth," I encouraged him.

"Well...." he half smiled. "Just between us...a maybe not."

"Um-hum, just like I thought," I nodded.

"Hey, let's just keep this between us though," Dr. Zhao smiled. "I need to be in cahoots with my colleagues."

I winked at him knowingly. "You got it."

"So you'll be at the dome in the morning, right?" Zhao asked, as they got up to leave.

"I guess," I shrugged, walking them to the door. "I don't think I have a choice."

"No, you don't," Dr. Zhao laughed, patting me on

the shoulder. "See you in the morning. Enjoy your tacos Airman Haley."

The next morning I walked alone into the dome dreading the day. As I pushed my way through the heavy door, Annessa greeted me almost immediately.

"Claire, I hope you're not mad at me," she said, grabbing me and hugging tightly. "Please don't be mad at me."

I hugged her back and smiled reassuringly at her. "Annessa, I'm not mad at you. I just wish you had told me. I wish someone had told me. I was completely blindsided and that was not fair."

She let go of her tight squeeze on me and looked me in the eyes. "I know, but honestly Claire, I didn't even know about it until two weeks ago. I thought I was here just for special training. I didn't know it would be anything like this."

I looked carefully around the empty dome, making sure there was no one else around before I spoke further. In the distance, I could hear male voices coming from one of the offices. I lowered mine to almost a whisper.

"Annessa, I don't think this is your fault at all. I just don't think it's safe for you and I'm worried. I'm deeply worried..."

"Claire, I'm fine. I promise," she interrupted. "And look!" She smiled, holding out her wrist. I gasped as I looked down at a faded Saturn ring tattoo on her left wrist. "It was there when I woke up this morning!"

I gulped as I lightly grabbed her wrist to get a closer look. Her tat was definitely there, but not as defined as mine and much smaller. "I don't know Nessa," I stammered. "It's pretty cool that you got the tat also, but I still think this is very unsafe."

Annessa rolled her eyes and smiled, but I could tell she was slightly agitated with me now. "Seriously Claire, I'm fine."

"But you don't know for sure. Just like I don't know for sure if I'm safe."

Annessa looked at me thoughtfully for a moment, then took a deep breath. "I don't care, Claire...and that's ok. Don't you understand? I would give up a thousand lifetimes just to be able to fly for even two minutes without ropes or a plane or a shuttle." She looked at the ground, gloominess stirring in her eyes. "Besides, what do I have to lose? It's not like I have a family or anything. The risk is worth it to me."

I stared at her, twisting the bottom of my shirt nervously. I knew arguing with Annessa was useless. She was like a doe eyed, innocent child and as obsessed with flying as I was. There was no getting through to her. The best I could do now was do my part in making sure she stayed safe.

I shrugged my shoulders. "Ok, Annessa. I'll do my part to keep you safe in all this, but I just want you to know where I stand."

"That's fair," she shrugged. "Thanks Claire."

"Alright, let's get these belays on Airman Clarence and get started," CMS Bryant commanded everyone.

I said nothing, but stood back as far as I could trying to not look as terrified as I was. Annessa looked over at me and smiled almost as if she was asking me if I was ok. I smiled back at her and winked. She was going through with this, so what good did it do to make her even more nervous than I'm sure she already was.

"Ok Hailey," Commander Whitley called, "we're gonna have you go up with her, walk her through everything and then maybe just be a backup if the ropes fail."

"Yes Sir," I said reluctantly, joining the group. So basically I was her safety net.

Got it.

"Ok," Annessa said, looking at me. "So yesterday I was able to get off the ground, but going where I want and landing has been a problem I don't know how to fix."

"Well, I learned to land on a big soft rug on my bedroom floor. I wasn't high in the air so landing wasn't as painful, so I suggest you learn that in a smaller setting As far as going where you want to go, it's all in your mind Annessa. I just focus on where I want to go and let my mind lead me."

She looked at me like she didn't believe me. "That's it? It's mind control?"

I shrugged. "It is for me. It's like walking. Your brain tells your body what to do and it just does it." Annessa looked at me even more confused. "I wish it were more technical than that so maybe I could explain it better," I said, "but it's not. That's pretty much it."

"Ok...well, let's do it," she said, as we both adjusted our radio headsets.

"Radio check," she said into the mike.

"I got you," I responded. "And me?"

"You're there," she said.

"I got you both," Commander Whitley chimed in as he, CMS Bryant and Dr. York took a few steps back from us. Annessa looked above at the dome ceiling and then suddenly shot into the air. I went up immediately after.

"Focus on where you want to stop Annessa!" I radioed to her as she rocketed higher.

"I am," she assured me.

I waited a few more long seconds. "Focus!" I said again with more urgency as the ceiling got a little too close to comfort for me.

"I am Claire!" she almost yelled.

I took a deep breath. What should I do? It didn't look like she was slowing down at all. I jetted closer, just in reach of her boot. I looked up past her at the rafters that were getting bigger with each passing second. Finally at what seemed to be the last moment, I grabbed her foot and began slowing us down to a complete stop. Annessa looked down at me, her eyes squinting in frustration.

"Really Claire?! What did you do that for?" she snapped,

as we hovered face to face, 6 feet from the ceiling.

"I'm sorry," I sassed back, putting one hand on my hip and pointing up. "I thought you were going through the skylight."

She rolled her eyes. "I told you I had it."

I bit my lip to keep from saying something I would regret. Two minutes into this whole experiment and I was already regretting being a part of it.

"Alright girls, come back down for a minute," Commander Whitley said into our headsets, breaking the awkward silence between us.

I looked at Annessa one more time before slipping straight down and landing softly in the middle big red circle. Everyone was quiet as I stepped aside to give her room to land. In the corner of my eye, I could see Jason step out into the dome from his duty post to watch her come down. I bit the bottom of my lip again nervously. This could be really bad. I prepared myself to jump and grab her should she lose control.

"Airman Clarence?" Commander Whitley radioed her. "Are you ok?"

"Yes Sir. I just need a minute please."

"Take your time," he reassured her.

We all waited for what seemed like forever, though it was actually just a couple of minutes. Finally Annessa radioed back.

"Ok, I'm coming down."

Every eye looked straight above as we held our breath. Annessa started out with a small drop of about 10 feet, then a mid-air pause. Another 10 feet, another pause. We all caught our breath when on the fifth try, she dropped 20 feet at lightning speed. I clenched my fist, readying myself to shoot off the floor and help her, but before I could blink, she had stopped again.

"I'm ok," she reassured us.

CMS Bryant looked at me, raising his eyebrows. I knew what that meant. Be ready to go. I nodded back to reassure him I was.

"Ok Annessa," I heard her talk to herself in our headphones. "You got this." She had made me pretty mad up there a bit ago, but I smiled in spite of that, because when I first started flying, I would quietly cheer myself on too.

Then next thing I heard was an audible gasp from the group. I glanced up to see Annessa slip effortlessly down to the ground and make an almost perfect landing. Everyone started clapping as they breathed a sigh of relief and I joined them, then I was quickly at Annessa's side to congratulate her.

"Good job girl." I said, giving her a quick hug.

"Thank you Claire!" she gushed. "That is the best feeling ever! I can't believe I can fly!"

I stepped to the side to let everyone else high five and congratulate her. Jason was clearly over the moon for her. He picked Annessa up, spinning her around. I stood back and watched them and in that moment thought of something weird. You know the movie *Toy Story*, right? When I was younger I probably watched that movie a thousand times and for some reason the face of Woody popped in my head. Woody, the old toy. The used up toy. I couldn't help myself, but I felt like Woody staring at Annessa, the brand new Buzz Lightyear.

SIXTEEN

THE NEXT TWO weeks, Annessa and I worked together side by side. Her flying power seemed to be developing stronger. Yes, there were a few glitches that I had to jump in and help out with, but for the most part she was almost as confident as I was. I busied myself trying to keep her as safe as possible, as I naturally felt she was my responsibility. Plus I was grateful for the distraction. I found out Johnny was unable to make it for Thanksgiving and my heart was broken.

On a bright, but crisp November Friday morning, we loaded into two vans to make our way out into the desert, just outside the base. We only went out a mile, because of the remote seclusion the area offered and also the cover the lookout towers provided. Everyone went out on this one, because today was a special day. We would be testing Annessa outside of the dome for the first time.

The two vans we took were bursting at the seams. One was full of every kind of equipment you could imagine, from radios to radars and even a drone for extra security. We all squeezed in the passenger van; Jason, Annessa, me, CMS Bryant, Commander Whitley, Dr. York, Dr. Zhao and the drone operator. Zhao had been forced to stay back because he had been nursing a serious cold and they feared it could harm Annessa's ability to fly safely.

"How are you feeling?" I asked Annessa as we waited alone in the van for all the equipment to be set up.

"I'm a little nervous," she said, tightening the straps to her parachute, "but I'm also so thrilled. I can't imagine rocketing up with nothing but blue sky ahead of me."

"It is the best feeling in the world," I agreed.

"Claire, I wish I didn't have to wear this stupid parachute. It's so heavy and unnecessary."

"Well, it isn't unnecessary Annessa. You need to wear it for at least the first few days until we know you're safe."

"But I have you," she joked.

"And I'll be there, but still...just keep the parachute on." I stopped for a moment and then gently grabbed her hand. "Annessa, I know I've been a little rough on you about all this, but please understand it's because I care about you and I want you to be ok."

"Aww Claire," she said, giving me a big hug. "I know that's what it is. It's actually nice to have someone who does care about me. I haven't had that in so long."

I paused for a moment. That broke my heart. I couldn't imagine not feeling like anyone cared about me. Maybe that was why Annessa felt like she needed this so much. Not for the thrill of flying, although that was enough within itself. Maybe it was for all the people fussing over her, looking out for her, making sure she was ok at all times, and the constant worry about her well being. In that way, all the attention is positive, especially if you are all alone in this world like Annessa.

"Well I do, so much," I smiled, pulling away from her and looking into her innocent blue eyes. "Please be careful and for goodness sake, focus!"

"I will," she laughed. "Thanks Claire."

Jason banged on the door, making us both jump. "Let's go girls."

"Seriously Jason?" I yelled at him and punched him in the arm as we climbed out of the van. "You scared us to death, loser."

Jason laughed, "Good! When I tell you girls to do something, you better make it happen!"

Annessa and I groaned at his lame attempt to have any authority over us.

"Keep on dreaming Jay," she laughed.

I stood on the side, watching as everyone worked on Annessa. Dr. York was checking her temperature and heart rate, while the drone guy checked her parachute one more time. Commander Whitley stood face to face with Annessa, pointing into the sky and giving her a perimeter of how far he wanted her to fly out. I turned on my radio to make sure I had verbal contact with her through all of this.

"...ok, so straight up and south is the safest range for you to fly," I cut in to hear him say. "500 feet max is the highest you can go and we'll let you know when you're there. Of course, if there's any issues with your chute, let us know immediately and we'll have Airman Haley there."

I gulped at the mention of my name and shivered at the thought of Annessa's life being in my hands. I didn't want to tell Annessa, because she was counting on me, but I felt like someone had their hands around my tummy and was squeezing the breath out of me. I was so nervous for her. I couldn't shake Major Silva's voice in my head reminding me of Major Kearney's death and how he had fallen out of the sky.

"You ok Claire?" I heard Dr. Zhao's calm voice beside me.

"Hey Dr. Zhao," I sighed, lifting up my mic so no one could hear me. "I guess, but just to remind you, I don't want any part of this...and just between us, I don't think it's fair to put her safety in my hands."

Dr. Zhao nodded quietly. "I definitely understand that sweetie, but we need you in this. She needs you. I don't agree with it either, but at the same time I know they need my expertise *and* since they're going to do it no matter what, we might as well help, right? I mean, especially if it helps you in the long run."

I smiled at him. Of course I knew he was right, but what a responsibility. "Thank you Dr. Zhao. I'll try to look at the bright side of it."

He smiled back and wrapped an arm around my shoulder, giving me a quick squeeze. "Yell if you need me ok?"

"Where are you going?" I asked, as he walked towards the van.

"I'm assigned to the control van," he said, rolling his eyes.

"Good luck with that," I laughed.

A cool brisk wind sent shivers down my back and I was glad when the sun peeked from the clouds a couple of minutes later, warming my face. I turned toward it, eager to zip into the sky closer to its warm rays.

"Alright everyone, let's do a check in," Commander Whitley instructed us.

I waited for the higher ups to check in first then it was my turn. "Airman Haley clear," I said loudly into my headset. I then double checked my strap to make sure it was secure in case I had to do a sudden take off.

"Ok Airman Clarence, we're ready when you are. Airman Haley, stay on the ground until further instruction," Commander Whitley said.

"Clear," I said, trying to hide the disappointment in my voice. Seriously though, wouldn't she be safer with me close by in the air? I guess Commander Whitley was too nervous to have us both in the air, but we had already been here an hour and I was getting antsy to fly.

"Commander Whitley from tower two," I heard an unfamiliar voice call.

"Go ahead tower two," he answered.

"Civilian aircraft at 31,000 feet, westbound."

I looked to the east and saw a dot of a plane way above the earth's surface, jetting across the sky and leaving a white tail behind it.

"Clear, thank you Sir," Commander Whitley said. "Ok, we go in two minutes."

I leaned back against the van and warmed myself in the sun's reflection. I watched Annessa for a moment trying to figure out her mood by her body movements. She rocked back and forth, a sure sign she was as nervous as I was.

"Ok Airman Clarence, we're clear," Commander Whitley said at last.

I took a deep breath as Annessa paused for a moment, then in the blink of an eye, shot high into the sky. My heart pounded in my throat and I squinted at her in the bright sun until she became invisible to the human eye. My fists clenched tight and I didn't notice until my fingernails began to hurt against my skin. I looked down at my tattoo that shimmered in the bright sunshine and my body tensed in anticipation of flying, but I had to wait for permission.

"Airman Clarence, do you copy?" Commander Whitley asked.

I stared into the blue sky trying to gain sight of her. She had shot up so high and so fast and was just gone. I didn't see her anywhere.

"Airman Clarence, do you copy?" he asked again.

The air waves were completely quiet. CMS Bryant and I exchanged worried glances.

"Airman Clarence, do you copy?"

Everyone remained eerily quiet for a moment, then before I could stop myself, I shot into the sky after her without waiting for their permission.

"Airman Haley, we're tracking her at ten thousand feet...looks like to the south and east of our location," I heard Dr. Zhao speak with urgency in his voice.

Ten thousand feet... how did she get there so fast?

"Clear, ten thousand feet, to the south east," I repeated, my voice breaking up with the wind hitting my mic. I had never flown this fast and this high before. Despite the flight-weather resistant suit and several layers I had on, my body began to shiver in the dense air.

I began searching desperately for Annessa, but the sky was so vast and the sun so bright, I had trouble seeing.

"She's at nine thousand feet," Dr. Zhao said.

"Claire, do you see her?" Commander Whitley's voice cracked through the radio.

"No Sir," I gasped as I changed direction and shot down head first, hoping to get under her for a better view. "Is her chute deployed?"

"No deployment detected," he answered.

I could feel my heart beating in my chest as I pushed all my weight down trying to gain speed, while frantically searching for any sight of her.

"Airman Clarence, do you copy?" Whitley asked.

Silence again.

"Airman Clarence, do you copy?"

"Annessa!" I yelled into my mic, breaking radio protocol. "Annessa, where are you!?"

"Seven thousand feet Claire, same location. We're trying to get a pinpoint," Dr. Zhao assured me.

"Well try harder!" I yelled back. "I can't find her!"

"Claire calm down," CMS Bryant snapped. "Try and get below the current location."

"She's below her," Dr. Zhao responded.

"Ok, keep flying down, but look up and see if you can find her."

"I'm looking," my voice cracked, as I started to tear up. "It's so clear today, why don't I see her?!" I flipped my body upright so I had a better chance of seeing her above. My eyes scanned the sky in desperation, back and forth, back and forth. Finally, by some small miracle, I saw her. She was at least a half mile away and plunging toward earth at such a high rate of speed, I didn't know if I could catch up.

"Oh my God! Oh my God! I see her!" I yelled, as I flew down and across the sky, chasing her as fast as my body could possibly go. "Deploy your chute Annessa!"

"How close are you Claire?" Commander Whitley asked.

"I'm at least a half a mile away," I gasped. "I'm flying so fast." I dove head first again, trying to push my speed even more, to no avail. I knew I was doing at least a hundred miles an hour as I did my best to control my breathing. Passing out at this speed was a huge possibility.

"Ok, we have you both on radar," the tower voice

boomed.

"Come on Claire!" I screamed at myself.

"One thousand feet," Dr. Zhao said, grimly.

I could see Annessa below me and more clearly now. She had definitely passed out. Her body spiraled out of control and she lay on her back. Her free fall to earth was much heavier and quicker than mine, because she had gravity working with her, while my body fought against it. Plus her heavy equipment was no help. I began to realize that no matter how hard I tried, the lack of gravity in my body was to my disadvantage now. The distance between us grew greater, though I was flying at full speed.

"She's passed out," I sobbed into the radio. "I can't get to her fast enough!" I screamed. "Annessa noooo!"

SEVENTEEN

I WOKE UP at three a.m. the next morning and looked around in the dim light of my room. For a brief moment all was calm and life was normal, until the horrific events of the day before flooded my mind. "Please be a dream," I whispered to myself as I rolled over, but I knew it wasn't. I had left the bathroom light on, because honestly I was too scared to be alone. The soft sound of snoring on the couch brought back more memories from the night before. Since I was so distraught, CMS Bryant had sent Zhao to my room to stay with me.

I slid out of bed and tiptoed quietly to the bathroom and gently closed the door. My head started spinning as my tummy cramped and I felt a wave of nauseousness consume me. I curled into a ball on my fluffy black shower rug as the grief hit at once. I sobbed quietly as images of Annessa filled my mind. After a few minutes, I heard a light tapping on the door.

"Claire?" Zhao said quietly on the other side.

"I'll be out in a minute," I replied, catching my breath and blowing my nose.

"No rush," he said. "I just want to make sure you're ok."

I took a few more minutes, then cleaned myself up and went into the living room where Zhao sat patiently on the couch. I curled up beside him and he placed his hand on my arm as I started crying again.

"Claire, I wish I could do something to help you feel better...you know this is not your fault, right?"

I slowly shook my head no. "If I had just gone up a minute sooner, I could have gotten to her Zhao."

He sighed and blew his nose, still nursing his head cold. "What were your orders, though?"

I looked at him knowing where he was going with this.

"Your orders?" he tried again.

I mumbled, "To stay grounded until...until..."

"Until further instructed," he finished for me. "So how is this your fault?"

"Because...because I knew better, Zhao. I knew something bad was going to happen."

Zhao looked at me sympathetically. "Claire, you have a superpower and it's flying, you are not, however, a fortune teller."

I slumped back on the couch. It was so sweet of Zhao to try and push the blame away from me, but there was no way I could clear my conscience of this. I wish I had done more. My heart ached so much for Annessa and I sobbed uncontrollably, while Zhao sat quietly beside me holding my hand.

"She didn't even have any family Zhao. There's no one to even notify."

Zhao sighed. "I know Claire. That's definitely heartbreaking."

We sat together in silence for a long while. I glanced at my friend arguing with myself about whether or not to share my secret plan I had made last night. I could see his eyes growing heavy, so I decided to hit him with it before he was out.

"Zhao," I said at last, "I'm getting out of here."

"What are you talking about Claire?" He mumbled, half asleep.

"I mean, I'm leaving."

Zhao sat straight up, wide awake now. "What? No you're not. CMS Bryant sent me here to watch you...are you trying to get us in trouble?"

"I'm not talking about tonight," I reassured him.

"Claire..."

"I'm gonna fly out of here and away from this place and all its horrible memories. Everything from now on is going to remind me of Annessa."

"That's a really bad idea Claire, you are still an Airman and property of the United States Air Force," he said sternly.

I shrugged, "Well, I don't care anymore Zhao. I want

to go home and be with my family and Johnny."

"Don't be crazy," he sighed.

I stared at Zhao, almost feeling sorry for him. He had gotten a tall order when they teamed him up with me. "I'm sorry Zhao," I said, putting my hand over his, "but I'm going. I've already made up my mind. I just thought I should at least let you know and not leave you blindsided."

He looked back at me and shook his head in disbelief, knowing I had made up my mind. "I swear Claire, you are too much." He looked down at the ground. "I feel like I'm never going to see you again. This time for sure."

"Oh Zhao, come on. You're going back to Hawaii tomorrow anyway, right?"

"Well yeah, but what does that have to do with anything?" he asked.

"If I'm getting out of here, where do you think I'm going?"

"You're not going back to Tennessee?"

I looked at him like he was crazy. "Seriously? Why would I fly into that hot mess? Kass said people there are looking for me everywhere."

He still looked confused. "So you're going..."

"Back to Hawaii. To my island."

"Claire, get serious."

"I *am* serious!" I said, emphatically. "I want to be totally alone. I just need some time Zhao and there's nowhere on earth I'd rather be."

Zhao rubbed his eyes in frustration. "Think about

what you're saying Claire. First off it's at least a seven hour flight from here..."

"I'll find a mountain to rest on," I argued.

"Food? Shelter?" he asked.

"I have my cave and my hammock still and I just need your help to sneak into the M.R.E. closet."

Zhao stood up and shook his finger at me. "Oh no missy, you're not dragging me into this one."

"You're already in this one," I said stubbornly, standing up beside him and folding my arms.

He stood quietly, rubbing his eyes again like he was getting a headache and I knew that headache was me.

"Fine, I'll get in the closet myself," I tried to compromise. "Just please don't tell anyone where I am. You should be on the plane and out of here Saturday before anyone even notices I'm gone."

Zhao stared at me for a moment, then finally threw up his hands in surrender. "Whatever Claire," he yawned.

"Thank you friend," I sighed, relieved.

"Come here," he said, wrapping me in his arms. "You are too much, girl."

The next morning I was called to CMS Bryant's office on the administration floor. I checked my eyes in my little face powder mirror on the way down in the elevator. They were puffy and swollen from crying and lack of sleep. Oh well. This is how I looked and that was that. I just didn't even care anymore.

"Good Morning Claire," his secretary greeted me then whispered, "I'm so so sorry about your friend."

"Thank you Grace," I gulped, pushing away the tears. She was always so kind.

"Command Master Sergeant is waiting," she smiled sympathetically.

I thanked her again, then walked into his office and stood at attention, half expecting everyone to be waiting. To my surprise, CMS Bryant was all alone.

"At ease and shut the door please," he instructed.

I closed the door quietly then found my chair directly across from him. I sat up as straight as I could, hoping that would keep my tears at bay. I hated crying in front of my command. I didn't want to be considered too wimpy and had worked so hard to gain respect with my fellow Airmen.

CMS Bryant stared at me for a moment before finally speaking. "I was going to ask if you slept well, but I can clearly see you didn't."

I cleared my throat. "No Sir I didn't, but it's ok because I'm wide awake anyway," I replied, a little more snarky than I had planned.

"Well, we've been extremely worried about you Claire and I just want you to know how sorry we are that you had to witness what happened."

I stared down, afraid to look him in the eyes. I knew I was going to lose it and I fought hard to hold myself together.

He continued, his voice softer. "We've been talking and think maybe it would be a good idea for you to see someone. We have a psychologist on hand in Houston and he's agreed to make himself available to you this week. But until then, you can take as much time as you need to heal from this..."

"I want to go home Sir," I interrupted before he could finish.

He looked at me wide eyed, a bit in shock. "Claire, you know that's not a possibility right now," he replied firmly, but I could tell he felt bad for me. "Our priority is still your safety. Clarksville is not a safe place for you right now."

I bowed my head and began rubbing my temples, trying to push away the headache that was now looming between my eyes.

He continued, "But...but I was wondering how you felt about maybe having your mom come for a little visit."

I shrugged. Of course I would love to have my mom here with me, but I had no plans to stay so it would be a waste to even fly her out. "Maybe after I get in a better place, Sir. I just don't want her to see me like this. She worries a lot...but thank you."

"Ok, that's fine. Whatever you need. I just want you to know we're here for you."

I thought carefully before I asked him what was on my mind. He must have sensed this because he asked me if I had any questions for him.

"Annessa...she didn't have any family?" I knew the

answer, but I was still hopeful that maybe there was someone out there.

"No," he sighed, "but her Command officer is looking deeper into it. We want to make sure before we have the memorial service this weekend."

"This weekend?" I repeated.

"Yes. Is that ok?"

I froze at the thought of a memorial service. It was more than I could handle. I got up and began pacing back and forth, tears filling my eyes again. "Excuse me Sir, but whose idea was this?" I stopped directly in front of him. "Because, whoever it was, they need to be fired immediately."

"Claire..."

"I told you guys this was going to happen!"

"Claire, sit down please," he commanded, softly.

I sat down in my chair again, arms crossed in defiance while tears slipped down my face.

CMS Bryant stood up and walked around to the front of his desk and had a seat on it, directly in front of me. "Believe it or not, this one was out of my hands, Claire. Dr. Albert, who you met at the crash site is the one who recruited Annessa. He and his higher ups. He was a part of Annessa's command. They are a relatively new special ops unit and were formed about six months after we discovered you. Annessa was chosen for obvious reasons already explained to you and she was more than willing, even with all the risks. But everyone here...well, we were just following government orders."

"But she was so young," I said, pushing through the lump in my throat.

"I know and trust me, I understand your hurt. I've lost three close friends in my line of work."

"You mean they were Airmen?"

He lowered his voice. "Claire, there are so many out of this world secrets the government keeps from the American people and many scientists have given their lives in pursuit of understanding the unknown. Your anti-gravity rocks aren't the only foreign mysteries to enter our atmosphere."

My eyes grew wide at what he was hinting at. He was basically saying what I knew to already be true from what I had seen and overheard around this base. Alien life did exist. I assumed he was just trying to distract me from my hurt over Annessa and I appreciated that, but it wasn't working. I still had to get out of here.

"Claire, go ahead and take the next few days off. I'll have Grace get in touch with the counselor and you can meet with him whenever you're ready."

"Thank you Sir," I said standing up and taking this as my opportunity to leave. I was going to get help, but it would be on my terms. I didn't need to talk to someone, I needed to get away and tonight at midnight I would be on my way.

EIGHTEEN

BY 11:30 THAT night, I had finished packing my small duffle. I brought as much as I could without weighing myself down. Flying with Kirsten had been a real challenge and I knew this flight would be much more difficult than that.

I rolled up one more sweat shirt and tucked it in with my clothes. I had enough M.R.E.s for a week, several pairs of sweats for the rainy nights, shorts, camis, a few bikinis and a bowl for catching fresh rain water. I brought my favorite flip flops and my black chucks I would wear in flight. In fact, my whole outfit was black to blend in with the night sky.

I was just finishing up when my phone rang.

"Claire?"

"Hey Zhao."

"You good to go?"

"Yeah, I'm going potty and then I'll take off."

He was quiet for a moment. "You know I hate it that I won't know you're safe for a few days."

"Zhao, I'm fine. I have to preserve my phone battery, plus I promise you I'll meet you at Waimanalo Beach for more supplies next weekend. You have my list, right?"

"I have it," he replied flatly.

"Ok, so Friday night, I'll fly to where I can get service so we can talk about everything."

"Ok," he sighed. "Claire, I'm worried about you. I don't want you to get in trouble for this."

"Thank you Zhao, but I kind of just don't care anymore. The consequences don't matter to me at this point and I just want out of here." I didn't mean to sound so abrasive, but I was so spent and just numb to it all.

Zhao sighed again. "This place is pretty lame. Are you flying off the top of the building?"

"No, just out of my window. That gives me less of a chance of being seen."

"Good idea," he agreed. "Claire, please be careful."

"I will Zhao. I promise I'll call you when I get to California. I'm going to rest there before I fly out over the ocean."

"Oh wow," he said, quietly.

"What?"

"That just sounds so amazing. Flying out over the ocean."

"I can't wait," I said, catching my breath.

We said good night and I took one final look around my room, checking to make sure everything was off and I had everything I needed. My phone charger sat on the nightstand. I decided to grab it just in case I could find a place to get a charge.

I pulled my warm black sweatshirt over my sleek ponytail and quietly opened the window. A cool wind blew in and the moon cast a bright glow on my side of the building. I looked down from my tenth story window and all seemed quiet and clear below. I had decided there was only one way to do this and that was to do it as quickly as possible. I strapped on my duffle, then slipped out of the window and hovered on the side of the building for a moment, as still as I could be. The moon looked neon white and a thick white cloud was approaching it from the west. Maybe I would wait a minute for it to slide over, so the sky wouldn't be as bright. I watched as it soon completely covered the moon, then closed the window and pushed off the window sill. I formed my body into a perfect diving pose, arms together and straight above, then shot into the air, rocketing in a straight line to get as high and out of sight as I possibly could. When I got at a safe distance in the air, I looked down at the base that was now just a small glow off the surface of the earth. I reached into my pocket and grabbed my skull cap and gloves, slipping them on since the sky was pretty cold at this altitude, then I set out to meet up with Interstate 10. All I would have to do is follow it and get to LA before the sun comes up, rest for the day, and then fly out tomorrow night at dusk.

Twenty minutes later, I was flying high above the runway-looking lights of I10. I settled in and began following them toward the west. This was the happiest I had been in so long. My favorite 80's hit list streamed from my earphones, as the stars in the sky sparkled bright above me. Every now and then, I would have to duck below the clouds so I wouldn't lose sight of my guide, but as soon as they lifted I was back up, eager to catch a shooting star or jet streaking above.

Around 3 a.m., I needed a potty break and spotted a large wooded area with a sliver of water running just to the south of the interstate. I flew out further away from the traffic below and into the darkness of the woods. The forest melodies grew louder and the thick fresh smell of nature enveloped me. I dropped just above the treetops, flying towards the shimmering stream that gurgled loudly in the darkness. The trees whizzed past and I finally landed just beside the stream in a clearing, where the moon cast a bright spot light through the shadows.

I dropped my duffle to the ground with a loud thud, eager to get the weight of it off for a while and grabbed one of my toilet paper rolls. I took care of business behind a tree, then found a low lying tree limb that hung out over the stream. It had a branch that was the perfect size for me to curl up in and rest. The night was so quiet and so peaceful, had I not taken that 4 hour nap today, I would have been out. My thoughts turned back to Annessa and my tummy turned into a knot as images of her raced across my mind. I almost felt guilty being here, enjoying this beautiful dark fairyland and she couldn't. I wish I could have done more to save her. "*I'm so sorry Annessa,*" I whispered, looking up into the heavens through the blowing leaves.

The sound of a stick cracking, interrupted my thoughts. I turned to see a doe slowly creeping up beside me. Her big brown eyes sparkled in the moonlight and she stopped just a few feet away staring a hole through me.

"I bet you're wondering what I'm doing here," I smiled at her. "Don't worry, I'm just passing through."

Much to my surprise, she made her way closer. I reached out my hand and slowly ran my fingers up her soft nose and she nudged in closer. Was this even real? What a sweet baby. Maybe she was hungry. I pulled a granola bar from my side pocket and fed her a bite. The sound of her chewing made me laugh and she nudged me for more. Before I knew it, we had gone through both of my granola bars and a baggie of grapes. I looked at the time. Three-thirty already. I had to move if I were going to make L.A. by dawn.

"Good bye beautiful," I said, petting her one last time, then strapped on my duffle as she ran off into the woods. I checked around one more time to make sure I had everything. Oops, my toilet paper. I tucked it in quickly, then shot off the ground and into the night.

Flying was exhilarating. It had been so long since I had been up this long. The flight to L.A. went by quickly and by four-thirty I was nearing the outskirts of the city.

My body was feeling the weight of the duffle now and I needed a place to rest before my flight over the ocean tonight. Still, I was pretty impressed with my endurance during this trip and only had to rest a couple of times; once on a tall building in downtown Tucson and once on a cliff off the side of a mountain.

I flew past the bright lights of L.A. and out over the ocean, looking for a safe place to land. Just to the south, the Santa Monica Pier stretched out dark and deserted into the tall waves that crashed below, spraying water high into the air. I set my eyes on the dark ferris wheel that was outlined eerily against the night sky and landed in a bright red passenger car at the very top. I breathed a deep sigh of relief as I unstrapped my duffle that pulled uncomfortably on my shoulders and let it slide off with a thud on the seat. I sat for a moment to catch my breath, then slowly peeked over the top looking for any activity below. A dock light directly beneath the ferris wheel was the only thing I had to work with and I couldn't see anything past its small glow on the boardwalk floor. I decided to sit for a moment and watch and listen, until at last I felt safe enough to come down.

"Well here goes nothing," I sighed and grabbed my duffle, then climbed over the seat. I paused for a moment to hear the waves pounding against the boardwalk, then dropped gracefully down, careful to avoid popping one of the thousands of ferris wheel bulbs and landed just outside the dock lights glowing circle.

A heavy mist covered the boardwalk as I walked

quickly toward the shore, in search of a hotel. Halfway down the beach sidewalk an open sign gleamed warmly into the night and I followed it into the quaint lobby of a small two story cottage hotel. This would be perfect.

I rang a tiny bell that sat on the counter and a smaller man, dressed like he just flew in from Scotland, soon appeared from the back room. He looked me over curiously as I did him also. I felt like I was in some kind of whimsical movie.

"Aye, may I help you young lady?" He asked in a thick Scottish accent.

"Yes Sir, I need a room please."

"Well, you're in luck, we have one more left after a late cancellation," he replied, opening his computer screen.

"Great. Thank you Sir," I said, relieved.

"You're traveling alone, then?" He asked.

"No Sir. My fiance will be joining me soon. He's running a few minutes behind." (I knew better than to tell any man I was alone.)

"Okay, I got you in room 4, just upstairs to the left. You have an ocean view."

"Perfect!" I smiled.

Thirty minutes later I was in my quaint, little room, freshly showered, in my warm pajamas and snuggled under the fresh sheets. Just before I fell asleep I turned my phone on for a minute just to text Zhao to let him know I was safe, then for the first time in the last week, rested without fear or anxiety.

The orange glow of the afternoon sun poured through the lace curtains and into my charming little room. I woke up to the chatter of voices, music, and just beyond that, the waves of the Pacific Ocean crashing against the shore. I slowly stretched and then slid out of bed and over to the window that was covered with bamboo blinds. I opened them to the smell of cinnamon and fresh baked bread. Below my window, people were busy shopping, while others whizzed back and forth on bikes, skateboards, and rollerblades. My tummy growled impatiently, as I looked at the clock. Five-thirty p.m. I should probably grab something to eat.

I piled my curly hair into a high bun and threw on a tee, my favorite denim shorts and flip flops. Outside the warm salty air enveloped me and I followed my nose to a hot dog stand and grabbed a corn dog and some lemonade. The Santa Monica pier looked like something out of a 1950's musical. I found a lone wooden bench to eat at and watch the sun go down. My heart was full as I sat in total contentment, eating the best corn dog I had ever had and watching orange and yellow sunbeams glistening off the waves. One of my favorite beach songs, *Amber* by *311* blared from somewhere behind me.

My ringtone suddenly interrupted my serenity and I looked down to see Zhao's name popping off my screen. Oh no. This was going to be bad.

"Hello?" I answered nervously.

"Claire?"

"Zhao?" My voice cracked. "Zhao, where are you?"

"I just landed in Hawaii, but Claire...Claire, I'm on my way to Lt. General Gray's office. I'm guessing they've already discovered you're gone. I have no idea what to tell them."

I sighed in frustration. I thought I would at least have a couple of days until they discovered I was gone. "Zhao, you can tell them the truth. You have no idea where I am right now...and...and you don't have to worry anyways, because I left a note."

"Claire!"

"I just said I'm ok and I'm needing some time alone."

He was quiet for a moment and then took a deep breath. "Ok...that's what I'll say then. Lt. General's not going to buy it though," he almost laughed, "but that's what I'll tell him."

"Zhao..thank you," I said. "Thank you, my friend."

"Yeah, yeah," he said dryly. "I'll hear from you Friday, right?"

"Friday," I confirmed. "And remember, my phone will be off this week. I don't want to be traceable.

"I remember," he sighed.

"Zhao...good luck."

" Yep," he laughed. "I'm going to need it."

I walked slowly back to my room, kind of feeling bad for putting Zhao in such a bad spot. I couldn't help it though, I reasoned with myself. Someone needed to know where I was and I already had a feeling they were tracking mine and Johnny's phone conversations, so it couldn't be him. Zhao had to be the one. I paused on the pier before going back into the hotel to gather my belongings and rest before take off. I needed to shut down my phone, since they knew I was gone and would probably be pinging it soon. I made sure my locator was off, then turned the power button off and watched as the screen faded to black. Any connection to anyone was completely gone now and somehow I felt ok with that. I felt safe with myself.

In my room, I gathered my belongings and layed on the bed to catch a quick nap before I flew out again. It was already seven-thirty and I had to make sure I was energized enough to fly for three plus hours with no rest. If I were lucky, I could find a small island or a cargo ship to land on, but there were no guarantees.

I fell asleep hard, my body still in flying hangover mode from the night before. At midnight the alarm by my bedside went off, waking me from a restless sleep. (I had dreamed about Annessa and could only remember flashes of it. I kept waking up, reminding myself it was only a dream, then fell right back to sleep.) I slowly dragged myself out of bed and grabbed all my belongings. My phone was at full charge and turned off and would remain so until Tuesday. I looked around the room one last time to make sure I had left nothing. Later today, if not sooner, I knew some government agent would be here snooping around to see if I had left any clue as to where I had gone. When I was fully convinced I had everything, I quietly closed the door and went down the stairs into the damp, foggy night.

The walk down to the end of the pier was gloomy and creepy. The dark shadows made the cartoon creatures and clown faces painted everywhere look like something out of a horror movie. I was glad when I finally made it to the very end. I glanced around to make sure I was alone, then dove off the dock and instead of shooting straight up, flew just above the dark water until I felt safe enough to go higher. Once I was out of any possible eyesight and the pier was a small flicker of light in the distance, I pulled out my compass and set off for my island. My heart skipped a beat as I flew at 20 feet above the white capped waves below and was even lucky enough to catch a school of dolphins jumping playfully below.

After a couple of hours the sky grew dark and I looked to the west where lightning popped and thunder rumbled in the distance. I could have sworn the weather said tonight would be clear. No worries though, I was less than an hour from the island. I paused briefly in the sky and pulled my hoodie up, then carefully slid my hand down the side of my duffle to try and grab my umbrella. I didn't dare unstrap it, because if I did it would be lost in the ocean for sure. The thunder shook the sky while I stretched my arm as far as I possibly could feeling for the handle.

"*Claire,*" I lectured myself. "*Seriously? How could you be so careless?*" I should have known not to pack it so far down. At last I felt the handle between my fingertips and tugged with all my might, pulling it out. I popped it up and took off again. The umbrella served as my windshield wipers, keeping the rain out of my face as I searched the pacific for my tiny island. This was proving to be more difficult than I thought it would be as the rain was blowing in sideways and the cloud coverage was blocking any moon light. I flew closer to the ocean's surface in hopes of seeing the tall cliffs light up as the lightning popped flashes against the shore line. Just as a little panic began to set in I heard the most wonderful sound; waves crashing against the jagged rocks, then the shimmering sound of them retreating. The lightning flashed again, lighting up the white beach below and I realized I was flying just to the north of it. I zipped down and above the palm trees, getting a scope of the island, then landed safely just outside of the mouth of my cave and scurried inside. My cave was so perfect, very dry and cozy. The heat of the day was still trapped in and I immediately dropped my bag on the smooth rock floor to catch my breath. I didn't realize how cold I was. My body trembled under my sopping wet sweatshirt and pants. I dug into my duffle and grabbed the large flashlight I had borrowed from the supply closet in Houston. It lit up the whole cave in an instant. I peeled the layer of clothes off, then hung them to dry on the two large branches

I had dragged into the cave over the summer. I threw on my bikini and then grabbed my water bowl to catch the fresh rain water, eventually filling up the four water thermoses I had. Finally, I dried off completely and put on fresh sweats and a tee shirt. The warmth of the cave enveloped me and I immediately felt exhaustion take over. My sleeping bag with the built-in pillow was so comfortable and I zipped myself completely up, opening the air vents on the side. I looked at my watch. Four-thirty a.m. I closed my eyes and soon fell asleep as the loud thunderstorm roared above. The next thing I knew I was waking up to a sunlit cave, ready to start my first day on the island.

NINETEEN

BY TEN THE next morning I was on the south side of the island, floating in the clear blue water just off the shore. The silence all around was so intoxicating and I laid on my back with my elbows in the sand holding me above water as the waves washed to shore around me. Two large birds that looked like some kind of crane soared above, eventually landing just to the west on the beach. They stood patiently looking into the water, trying to catch their lunch. I watched them curiously and they returned my stare. I knew just what they were thinking. "*What is she doing here?*" They were so beautiful.

That evening I walked the shore of the whole island picking up some unique shells to make necklaces and charms for my sisters. The tiny ones were my favorite. They came in all colors and had a pearl-like finish inside.

At dinner time I grabbed my first M.R.E. and opened it. I had this one before at Campbell. It was a Tuna Mac, which wasn't bad at all, but I didn't care anyway. I was so hungry. I ate and then sat at the west end of the island watching the sun go down. The contrast between the ocean and the sunset colors were stunning and they eventually melted into each other as the sun disappeared behind the water. I stayed even longer as the moon moved over my little bay and the stars began to appear. I felt so much peace here and although I knew I was going to be in a lot of trouble when I went back, I also knew I was right where I needed to be.

That night I grabbed the brush and bamboo I had gathered during the day and made a makeshift bed for my sleeping bag and a tiny fire pit in my cave. I curled up with one of my books and began a series I was excited to start. But by 10, I was fast asleep, only seven chapters in and the flames from my campfire now just glowing embers.

The next few days were paradise. I kept myself busy swimming, making island jewelry, reading, cliff diving and taking a few night flights. Wednesday night the moon was bright, so I took a short flight out to the southwest of the island. I wasn't looking for anything in particular. I just wanted to fly. I dreamed of a life where I could fly anytime I wanted, without fear of being seen and being able to fly in the daytime. I paused when I got about 200 feet up and layed on my back for a while, looking up at the heavens and thinking about Annessa. I kind of felt bad for missing her memorial service, but at the same time I don't think I could have gone even if I were there.

Below me a loud groan came out of the ocean. I looked down to see a large blue whale shoot out of the water and plunge back in, causing a large wave of water to ripple away from him. Immediately another one emerged, her massive fin rising off the ocean's surface and then disappearing below. I dropped straight down and realized a whole family of whales were playing together in and out of the water. I was close enough to feel the water spray up on my legs as they splashed around and I sat in a chair position, my legs dangling in the air. I had to be the luckiest girl in the world.

Friday night I went up again for the third time that week, only this time I was on a mission. I had to find an area with service, so I could talk to Zhao. We were going to make a plan to meet at our rendezvous place for more supplies and just to check in. After flying north toward the Hawiian islands for about twenty minutes, I was finally able to pick up a signal.

"Claire?" Zhao answered.

"Hey Z," I said happily. It was so good to hear his voice.

"Oh my goodness girl. I've been waiting for your call! Where are you?"

I looked around at the black sky. "Ummm...somewhere over the Pacific."

Zhao laughed. "Man, I'm so glad you're ok."

"Zhao, I told you I would be fine," I reassured him. "How's everything?"

"It's fine. They're looking for you, of course."

I sighed. "I kind of figured they would be."

"Well what do you expect, Claire? You're like a secret government treasure and a lot of curious minds would love to get their hands on you."

That made me pause. I heard it a lot more lately. "Maybe," I agreed, "but you know what Zhao? I'm tired of hiding from everyone. Being on my island and getting to fly anytime I want is like a dream. If I have to hide the rest of my life, what's the point? I tried it their way and now I want to try it mine...I just don't want to get you in trouble."

"Yeah, I understand Claire. Lt. General said he knows I know what's up, but he doesn't want to bring me into all of it."

"Wow, that was nice of him," I said, relieved. "I've been worried about you in all of this Zhao."

"Well I'm fine," he assured me. "You just stay safe up there."

"I will," I smiled. "What time are we meeting up tomorrow?"

"Let's go for 10 p.m.?"

"That works for me...and you got my list?"

"Oh yes," he laughed. "It's going to be fun buying all your girly stuff at Walmart tomorrow. Face lotion? Really Claire?"

"The sun's drying out my skin," I almost whined.

"Whatever. Anyway, you better get off here and shut your phone down. I'm sure they're pinging it."

"Okay Zhao," I said. "Good night."

"Good night trouble," he laughed.

Saturday evening, just as the sun was setting at dusk, I flew off the island enroute to Waimanalo, a small beach town on the island of Oahu and a forty five minute drive from Hickam. We made a plan to meet at a little cafe, just off the coastline. I decided to get there an hour early so I could charge my phone and just unwind.

At exactly 9:05 I landed on the dark beach where a patch of tall palm trees blocked my landing from the main coastal road. The village was right down the road, so it would take me just a few minutes to walk there. As I neared the lights, the air came alive with the sound of tourists and locals, shopping the many shell shops and eating on the patios of various restaurants. Live music poured from a tropical bar and people danced on the deck outside as I walked past. It smelled so amazing here, like cheesy, oniony, garlic fresh bread and sweet caramel popcorn all combined. I stopped at the little variety store and bought a bag to take back with me to the island, as well as a cute little earth tone bikini with a matching wrap skirt. I was thankful I had pulled out plenty of money at the coffee shop A.T.M. on the base before I left. One swipe of my debit card and they would know in an instant where I was.

I found the Island Cafe toward the end of the main shopping area on the west side of the road. I requested a table near an outlet to charge my phone and was lucky enough to get one overlooking the ocean. My tummy growled angrily at me, as I had purposely skipped my M.R.E. dinner so I could pig out on some real food. I ordered a large plate of seafood taco salad, (yes that's a thing) and waited patiently for Zhao to show up.

At ten on the dot, Zhao walked through the island beads that hung in the doorway to the patio. I stood up to greet him and he immediately came over and wrapped me up in his arms. It felt amazing to be hugged. I didn't mind being by myself, but it could get a little lonely after a while.

"Wow Claire, you really look great," he smiled looking me up and down. "I wasn't expecting this at all."

I stared at him a little confused and amusingly insulted. "What's that supposed to mean?" I asked, giving him the squinty eye as we sat down.

He lowered his voice. "You're staying on a deserted island. I was expecting your clothes to be tattered and you to smell bad at least."

"Oh my goodness Zhao," I laughed. "This isn't *Cast Away*. It's like camping out."

"Well, how are you taking a shower?'

"Well if you must know, nosey, in either the ocean or if it rains I'll wash my hair with the water pouring from the large palm leaves."

"Oh Claire, that sounds miserable."

"No way," I sighed. "It's incredible there Zhao."

I spent the next twenty minutes answering all of his questions about the island. What did I do there all day, am I eating enough food, did I feel safe and what kind of wild animals were hanging around. I answered all his questions as thoroughly as I could and did my best to describe my island and put his mind at ease. (There's no wild animals, by the way.) By the time I was done, he was staring off in the distance wishing, he said, he could go back with me.

"Well, I got an interesting text this week," he said, snapping out of it.

"Oh really? Who?" I asked, taking a slice of the pizza he had ordered.

"Johnny," he replied, looking at me curiously.

Ok, I wasn't expecting that. "Johnny?" I repeated.

"Yeppers."

"What did he say?" I asked, wide-eyed. "Is he mad?"

"Well...yeah. I mean, he wants to know where you are."

I nodded in silence. "Well...what did you tell him?"

"I told him I don't know...because honestly, I don't know. I don't know where your island is."

I put my pizza back on my plate. I had suddenly lost my appetite.

"It's ok Claire," Zhao said, taking my hand. "He understands why you left. Apparently, Major Silva found out about what happened with Annessa and he's not happy about it at all. He said you should have never been put in that position."

I nodded my head in agreement. Major Silva always had my back.

"I want to call him so bad Zhao, but I can't. They'll..."

"I know. They'll track your phone," he finished for me. "I told him that too. I told him wherever you are, you'll give up your location if you call him and he agreed with that."

"Thank you for that, Zhao."

"One more thing," Zhao smirked.

"Ok."

"He said he loves you and to contact him as soon as you possibly can."

I smiled. Knowing he still loved me and was thinking of me made the butterflies in my tummy flutter in relief. Sometimes I wondered when he would just say enough is enough with me. We had been together almost three years now and had probably been in the same city as each other less than half of that time.

When my phone was done charging, Zhao and I packed up the leftover pizza and strolled down the little boardwalk. It was almost empty now as the midnight hour was fast approaching.

"So you'll meet me here at the same time next Saturday, right?"

"Of course," Zhao smiled, looking down at me. "And you'll check in with me on Tuesday."

"Of course," I echoed him.

Zhao wrapped me up and gave me the best hug ever. I think he knew I needed it. I had just spent the last hour talking his ear off and he had mentioned he could tell I was in need of some human contact.

We soon parted ways, him to the parking lot just east of the shopping district and me into the thick jungle brush and the dark beach. Luckily the moon peeked out from behind the clouds for a minute so I could find my way.

I strapped on my backpack of goods Zhao had brought for me and walked to the water's edge looking one more time to make sure there was no one around before shooting over the ocean's surface. A mile out, I made a sharp turn upwards and then south to start my flight towards my new home.

That night I snuggled under the new soft blanket Zhao had got me. I didn't request it, but he was just so thoughtful that way. It would give me an extra layer of warmth on the rainy nights in my cave. I thought about my night and how much fun I had with Zhao. I had been a little worried showing up on the mainland, especially since the whole media thing on the beach, but we blended in just fine.

Or so I thought we did.

TWENTY

WHILE I WAS soaking up the sun on my island in the Pacific, my mom sat and worried under the gloomy, winter clouds in my hometown of Clarksville. Major Silva had filled her in on what was happening in my world, but we hadn't talked since the weekend before everything went down and now that was almost four weeks ago. Time had passed so quickly on my island and I couldn't believe I had already been here two weeks. I had been so consumed in my own plight, I didn't realize my family would be so stressed. I knew my mom had Major Silva in her life now, so I just assumed he would be letting her and Kass know everything was ok with me, even though he was unsure himself. I wish I would have been more thoughtful of them.

Kass came home from school the second Wednesday

I had been AWOL, to find mom sitting on the couch in silence. My mom did her best to cover up and shield us from any kind of drama, but on this day it was too obvious. Kass sat down beside her and held her hand while my mom made an attempt to smile and reassure her everything was ok.

"Mom, have you heard anything lately?" Kass asked quietly.

"Not since Sunday, honey. Silva called and said they know she's ok, they just have to find her."

Kass sighed. "Mom, maybe she just doesn't want to be found for a while. And after what happened, I don't blame her."

"I understand sweetie, but I would just like to hear from her, just to know she's ok."

"Yeah," Kass agreed with her. "Me too mom."

It's funny how things happen. Some may call it intuition, but I call it a God thing. For some reason that night on the island, my family was heavy on my mind and I decided to make contact with them. I flew to my hotspot twenty minutes north of the island and powered my phone on. I scrolled down to Kass' number, because I thought they would be more likely to bug mom's phone than hers. Then I sent a simple text.

"I'm ok. I love and miss you guys and I'll be home soon."

Kass would later tell me that text changed everything for mom. She stopped stressing and was able to return to her normal self. She also shared it with Alicia, like I knew she would.

I thought about my Mony all the time, as she was busy getting ready for her wedding and I was missing it all. Shawn and her had purposely moved it to the spring, just to make sure I could be there. Now we were just a couple of weeks to Christmas and I worried I wouldn't make it back to Clarksville for a very long time. When they caught up with me this time, I was sure I would be going to some tightly locked government jail facility, where they would lock the door and throw away the key. I trembled thinking about it 50 feet above sea level that night, as I waited for Kass' reply back to me. At last my screen lit up with her return text.

"Claire! Oh my goodness girl! We've been so worried!"

"I'm so sorry to worry you both. I can't text for long, but please tell mom I will contact her soon. I'm completely safe."

"Ok, mom is here. She said , "please be safe, come home soon, check in with us and we are praying for you."

"Thank you both so much. I love you all."

"We love you too and we'll see you soon."

I loved her comment and then immediately shut my phone off. I hung in the air for a moment, then decided to head back. I was just a few minutes into flight, when I heard in the distance the familiar sound of a jet engine slicing through the night. They must be doing night exercises from the base, I assumed. I looked behind me in time to see it streak across the sky close to where I had just been. Good thing I had gotten out of the way in time. I was pretty sure I was too little to be picked up on radar, but at this point, who knows what the U.S.

military had up their sleeve.

That Friday evening, Zhao and I met for our usual weekend date and decided to stroll the boardwalk for a while. I didn't want to go back to the island right away and since Zhao had no obligations the next morning, he was ok with that. The whole street was decorated with Christmas lights and lit up palm trees. Hawaiian Christmas music poured over the street speakers and every now and then we would stop at a shop when something caught my eye. I had begun to buy small Christmas presents for my family in case, by some lucky chance, I would be able to be home by then.

"So Claire, what are your plans now?" Zhao asked as I paused to look at a ukulele playing Santa Claus ornament. My Kass would love this.

"My plans..." I said, confused.

"Your plans after the island? You've been away for almost three weeks now. You can't stay there forever, you know."

I sighed as we headed inside the cute little shop to pay for my ornament. Michael Buble's *"It's Beginning To Look A Lot Like Christmas"* filled the air, mixed with the smell of sweet cinnamon and vanilla. "I don't know Zhao. I'm not ready to go back to the compound."

"Who says you have to go back there? I'm going to ask if you can stay here in Hawaii with me."

I smiled up at my friend. "Thanks, but honestly I just want to go home. These past six months have been crazy. The only good thing that has come out of it was meeting you."

"Well, I know that's true," Zhao winked. "Have you made contact with Johnny?"

I paused in the back of the cozy shop to look at some miniature Christmas trees. "Well, I did send him a text on Monday, just to let him know I'm ok, but he hasn't texted me back yet."

"Maybe he didn't get it," Zhao defended him, picking up a little snow covered tree. "Maybe they can't get texts from you there."

I bit my bottom lip, a little frustrated at the thought of it. "Mom and Kass got my texts," I shrugged.

"Claire..."

"I'm sorry, it's just a little frustrating sometimes."

"Well, you need to give him a break," he said softly, "I mean.. I love you, but you're no cake walk."

I gasped and gave him a little shove. "What are you guys...like best buds now?"

"No," he laughed, heading toward the register. "We just talked for a bit."

"You didn't tell me you talked, *talked* to him," I said, following close behind him. "What did he say to you?"

"Mind your business, Claire," he laughed, putting my ornament on the counter and pulling out his wallet.

I stared at him curiously. He was acting really weird.

"No, I'm paying for it," I argued, reaching for my

wallet.

"Can't use your card," he smiled, holding his debit card in my face and then inserting it before I could protest.

"Really?" I said under my breath, while the white bearded chubby guy behind the counter smiled at us. "Thank you, Sir," I smiled back. He looked like a tropical Santa in a Hawaiian shirt.

I followed Zhao outside, where a cool breeze flowing down the wooden sidewalk caught me off guard. I shivered and threw on my hoody.

"Let's stop in here and finalize plans for the week," Zhao said, pointing at the coffee shop.

I followed him inside and we grabbed a small booth in the corner, each of us ordering a hot chocolate with a peppermint stick.

"Ok, so you're going to call me on Tuesday night?" he asked.

"Yes Sir," I replied, blowing my nose with my napkin.

"Claire, are you ok?" His eyes squinted at me. "Are you keeping warm on that island? I would think it would be chilly at night."

"Oh Zhao, you don't have to worry about that," I reassured him. "You'd be surprised how much just flying south of here can make a difference weather wise."

Zhao stirred his hot chocolate with the peppermint stick. "I'm just worried you're going to get sick or get hurt and I won't know and won't be able to get there to help you. I just...I just really think you should turn yourself in soon."

I sat up straight in the booth chair. "Turn myself in? Zhao, I'm not a criminal."

"I know," he quickly reassured me and lowered his voice, "but you know, you are AWOL." I nodded quietly, staring down at my mug as the realization of what he was saying hit me. "I'm sorry, I don't mean to scare you."

"No, you're right," I agreed. "I'll think everything over and let you know on Tuesday what I'm going to do."

"Well, you know I'm on your side no matter what you decide, right?" he said.

"I know Zhao," I sighed. "I don't know what I'd do without you."

Zhao and I hugged quickly under the streetlight that lit the path to the beach.

"Ok, I'll be waiting to hear from you Tuesday and not a minute past eight, because you know how I worry."

"I know," I giggled. "I promise."

I slipped on my winter hat and gloves and he squeezed me one more time. The night air wasn't cold by any means, but the higher I flew, the more crisp the air grew and I definitely needed the extra protection.

Tonight I didn't wait to get to the beach to take off. Instead, I flew to the top of the palm trees and directly over the ocean. The night was so black, I had no worries about being seen.

Fifteen minutes later, I was rocketing over the Pacific,

eager to get back to my island. I had just passed over the halfway point (a small dot size island directly below), when I felt a gush of wind and a sensation I could only describe as some sort of wave of energy push me forward. It felt like someone had shot me out of a cannon and my body hurled forward in an out of control spin through space. It took a minute, but I was able to eventually take control again and I looked above to see some sort of jet streaking across the sky. I hung mid air watching it fly a couple of miles out, then quickly turn to the west in a small half circle and head back...wait a minute...was it? It was headed directly toward me again. I froze in the sky, my eyes wide and unsure of what it was doing. The jet moved toward me at lightning speed and I kept still, not knowing if I should move up or down to avoid it. The pilot aimed the nose right at me and came within fifty feet, this time directly above.

The vacuum from the jet sucked me down and I began falling toward the earth, on my back, with my arms and legs flailing. I looked up and watched in horror as the pilot again did a 180, clearly searching the sky for me.

I immediately curled myself up and cannonballed toward the water. I had to find a place to hide. The island I had just seen flashed in my mind and I backtracked just above the ocean for about a mile, until I at last found it.

This island was so small and so dark. From what I could tell it was maybe 3 square blocks with a tiny, barely there beach. I landed softly in the sand and looked around. The thick island brush had grown over and onto the sand and the long vines from the tropical forest snaked their way down parts of the beach to the water. Behind me I could hear a branch snap and I ducked down close to the sand to see where it came from. The wind blew hard through the palm leaves, making a soft noise that sounded like a long *shhhh*.

I looked into the dark sky in search of the jet, but it was long gone. What was that dude's problem? Obviously he saw me and obviously he was looking for me, but he almost killed me in the process.

I stood up and shook the sand off my jeans. I was just about to lift off when a familiar popping sound shook the sky and vibrated in my ears. A Black Hawk seemed to come out of nowhere and was now racing toward the island. I jumped up from the sand and scurried behind a large palm tree, getting as close to the ground as possible. A bright spotlight cast a perfect, large white circle across the surface of the water and then to the beach, zipping back and forth in search of something and I had a feeling that something was me.

I stayed low to the ground, covering my head in my arms as the helicopter kicked up wet sand, the wind spraying it all over me and into the jungle. It's mighty blades pounded so loud in the night, I had to cover my ears and stay as still as possible, hoping they would give up soon. But they didn't. The next thing I knew, a marlow rope was dropped down and ten soldiers quickly descended. I pressed my back up against the thick palm tree and then quickly flew up and into the large branches.

Tucked deep into the palm leaves, I waited anxiously for my opportunity to fly out. Above, I could hear the jet reapproaching and below, the surprising sound of a ferocious dog bark. I looked down at the dog who was now standing on two legs at the bottom of my tree, barking hysterically, as the jet passed overhead, almost as if to remind me they were still on my trail.

"What do you think?" I heard the soldier with the dog yell to his buddy, then shine his flashlight up.

"Dude, do you seriously think she's going to be hiding in trees? This chick can *fly*! She's probably halfway to Australia by now."

The first guy shrugged, pulling the dog down. "Well, let's at least finish looking so we can tell Major we did what we were asked."

I froze up in the tree. Major? I wonder which Major they were referring to. I wondered if he knew one of his jets almost took me out tonight. I bit my lip in frustration. I had to get out of here now.

Very quietly, I lifted myself out of the palm branches, sticking my head up just enough to get a birds eye view of the copter. It hovered, waiting patiently for the troops to return, but I was not. I decided my best choice was to fly from tree to tree to the other side of the island, then directly north and just above the water. My island was south, but I figured if I could get far enough away, I could fly west and make a big half circle back to my island.

The trees were swaying wildly and a light rain began to fall as I finally made it to the other side. There was no beach here, just brush and trees that grew right up to the edge of some small rock walls. I pushed myself off the tree, then straight down to the water's surface and as fast as I could, flew out over the ocean. My teeth chattered against the brisk wind and rain that was now hitting my wet, sand drenched clothes, thanks to the big drops of dew on the palm trees.

I was careful not to fly too far north and made a sharp turn toward the west. The helicopter was now just a small dot of light against the dark sky and the jet long gone, when I felt it was safe to return to my island.

My body felt like jelly as I touched down in front of my cave. I went inside and pulled the brush door I had made closed, as thick drops of rain began splattering against it. Pulling my dirty hair into a high bun, I cleaned myself with wet wipes, threw on some warm jammies, and laid on my new "bed" which was made from some sticks and vines I had woven together the first week I was here. (Not to brag, but it was actually a pretty nice one too. It set a good two feet off the ground and was as solid as a rock. I left the middle hollowed out and had filled it with soft palm branches that had to be changed out weekly, as they became hard and brittle. My thick sleeping bag laid on top of that and it was one of the most comfortable beds I had ever slept in. I was pretty proud of it and had even turned my phone on for a moment just to get a few pics to show Kass later.)

I immediately fell asleep, dreading the fact that this could be my last week on the island. After tonight, I knew something had to change. This Major guy was getting seriously close to finding me and apparently knew exactly what he was doing.

TWENTY-ONE

THAT SATURDAY MORNING I slept until almost 10. By the time I woke up the cave was toasty warm. Outside I could hear seagulls squawking at each other as they dove into the shallow water in search of a midmorning snack.

I scooped up my bath products, then flew to the south side of the island to see if there was any water in the large bowl I had made of palm leaves. With all the rain we had overnight there should be plenty.

On the south beach, my palm bowl sat on a large flat slab of rock that stuck out from the sand. The rock not only kept the bowl from flipping over, but the heat from the rock kept the water warm. I grabbed my cup and started washing my hair, cleaning out the leftover sand from last night and adding extra conditioner to tame my frizzy curls. I used the rest of the water and soap to scrub my body and shave the best I could, but I didn't worry too much knowing I would be right back in the ocean before the day was over. The sun was almost directly above, when I finally slipped on my new crocheted bikini and flip flops. I looked up at the sun, shielding my eyes through my John Lennon shades. It looked like it was almost noon and since my tummy was growling in protest, I knew it had to be. I slid on my soft cotton shorts and cleaned up my mess, then flew back to the cave to grab lunch. Zhao had given me some new MRE's as well as non perishables from the store. I settled on making a peanut butter and jelly sandwich and had an orange with my water.

I grabbed my towel and backpack then flew back over the jungle to picnic on my towel spread over the rock. I peeled my orange and watched dolphins playing just beyond the breaking point. They jumped in and out of the water, talking and chasing each other. They looked like they were having so much fun together and I was almost envious of them. Maybe I was getting a little lonely here.

The sun warmed the rock so much, I started getting toasty and decided to cool off in the water. Zhao had bought me a little snorkeling set from Walmart, because he thought I might "get bored" on the island, so I decided to give them a try.

I piled my freshly washed hair into a high bun (I knew my clean hair wouldn't last long) and walked down the west side of the island, where I had seen what looked like a coral reef. I put the snorkels on and took a practice breath. I had never done this before, but it didn't seem like it could be that hard. I flew out over the ocean, just to make sure it was safe. The water was crystal clear and just below the surface I could see brilliant colors reflecting off the sunbeams shooting through the water.

I slipped into the Pacific and started my snorkeling adventure. Why I had never done this before, I'll never know, but it was one of the most exciting and beautiful things I had ever seen.

The water sparkled all around me like a thousand diamonds, while bright colorful fish swam around, seemingly unbothered that I was even there. I glided through the corral tunnels and around bright tropical plants, careful not to touch anything and careful to not let my snorkel slip under the water. A couple of times, I held my breath to dive a little deeper and get a better view of something that caught my eye. I didn't know much about the reefs, but I did remember reading about the human destruction of them. This particular reef was so beautiful and unbothered, I didn't want to do anything to mess that up.

I don't know how long I was in the water, but it was quite a while. I had pretty much swam around the whole reef and was just finishing up exploring the southern tip of it, when a loud splashing sound to the east caught my attention. I poked my head up and looked around. Something thrashed violently back and forth causing a white foam wave to roll out towards me. I took my goggles off to get a better look, but by this time the water's surface was calm again. That was weird.

The sun was now casting a hazy orange glow all around me. I looked up at the clouds that had waves of orange colors popping off a bright blue sky. I floated on my back watching in awe as they changed shape and size, one even looking like a puppy's face.

Suddenly, a jolt on my left thigh spun me around. From the corner of my eye, a large gray fin sliced quickly through the water. I caught my breath and turned to see where it was, but it was gone.

"Ok Claire," I said, grabbing my mouth piece that had floated a little bit from me, "you're outta here."

Then he was there. All I remember seeing was hundreds of white teeth behind two flaring nostrils and large dark eyes. The Great White charged toward me and I instantly flew backwards, dodging him just in time. Behind me, I felt the current shift around my legs and another one surfaced. I looked up and quickly shot out of the water, just as he dove at my legs. Had I been a split second longer, he would have completely bit off the bottom of my right leg.

I hovered over the water counting out loud; one, two, three, four large sharks! They swam aggressively in a circle, seemingly agitated by my disappearance, but I very soon realized it wasn't only me they were after. A little dark head peeked up from the surface of the water, as it swam desperately toward shore not far from us. A small sea lion was bobbing in and out of the water, barking for help and swimming for its life. I watched from above as one of the sharks turned his attention from me and toward the poor little guy.

"No!" I yelled at the sea lion. "Quiet!" But he continued crying even louder. I had to do something. I flew quickly toward him, checking over my shoulder as the shark's fin rose in and out of water, stalking his prey. My mind scanned every memory I had of sharks and what little I had been taught about them. I had always heard you were supposed to punch a shark in the nose if attacked, but by the size of this guy, I didn't think that would affect him much.

The shark disappeared deep beneath the water as we approached the sea lion. I knew what that meant. A surprise attack from underneath. I did the only thing I could do and as quick as a flash, swooped down to rescue him. I scooped him up, placing my arms underneath his tummy and flappers and lifted him out of the water just as the shark's fin shot up in front of us. The sea lion barked in fear as we rose higher and higher above the ocean's surface. We both looked down to see the great whites splashing around in agitation.

The little guy squirmed in fear and I held onto him for dear life.

"It's ok buddy," I reassured him. "I'm going to take you somewhere safe." Believe it or not, me talking to him seemed to calm him down and he stopped shaking as much. He made the cutest little baby sounds and my heart just broke for him. His mom had to be around here somewhere.

I flew quickly back to the beach and set the little fella down on my beach towel, then grabbed my phone to get some video of him. I had been recording everything I could for my family. I wanted them all, but especially Kass, to experience what I had. I felt so bad for not being home her senior year, so I thought this might make up for it a little. I had tried to explain it, but it just wasn't the same as seeing it.

As of right now, I had so much footage on my phone; everything from my rescue mission with Kirsten, to Zhao, to Annessa and some midnight flights over the ocean. Now I could add all my island adventures to that list, including my bed and all the cool stuff I had made.

"Look at my new buddy you guys! Isn't he so cute? I just saved him from a pool of Great Whites!" I narrated into my phone. "I was just swimming and they came out of nowhere...and don't worry mom, I saw them in time," I laughed, half telling the truth. "But anyway, I'm praying I find his mom in time."

As if he knew what I was saying, the little sea lion tipped his head completely back and was looking at me upside down. He smiled in what I believe was a moment of gratitude and I kissed his cheek in the camera.

That night I lay in bed by the fire, finishing up a new series I had been reading about sea life, of which the last two chapters were oddly enough about Great Whites. Luckily, around twilight, my little buddy's parents had showed up just offshore to get him. They barked at me from the safety of the water, while he eagerly swam out to meet them. That was a huge relief, because I didn't know how he would do sleeping in the cave with me, but I was willing to try.

I closed the book and stared at the glowing cave ceiling. Tomorrow would be Sunday and soon I would have to decide how much longer I was staying on the island. I dreaded having to face the higher ups, but I also longed to reconnect with my family and Johnny. I was so tired of being away from them and had made up my mind no matter what, I would not go another day without them in some remote base out in the middle of nowhere. Life was too short and I was not going to hide anymore.

My mind was full, planning what I would say to Lt. General Gray and how they would respond, but soon all the sun and salt water began to catch up. I drifted off into a peaceful sleep and slept so soundly, I missed the light rain and thunder echoing outside the cave. I missed the sound of crashing waves against the rock wall and beach, but most importantly, I missed the grinding motor of a boat in the Pacific, fighting through the waves and heading straight toward my little island.

Before I even opened my eyes, I felt their presence. I was

sound asleep, but somehow just knew something was off. My eyes popped open wide to three tall, dark figures looking over me, their faces covered in camouflage makeup and black skull caps. I blinked twice hoping it was a dream, but all too quickly realizing it wasn't. I gasped in terror and before I could even move, a bongie cloth was placed over my mouth and I was flipped on my stomach. In one swift motion my hands were tied behind me and my feet bound. I screamed through the cloth and tried kicking back with my bare feet, but to no avail. They both grabbed and carried me to the mouth of my cave, bumping my head and shoulder along the way. It was then that I saw the others. At least a dozen or more armed with rifles entered the cave as we went out.

Outside, the cold rain stung against my bare skin and I shivered as lightning flashed across the sky and lit up the beach. With each flash I desperately scanned their bodies to see if they were wearing military uniforms or had any rank or unit insignias, but couldn't see any in the poor lighting. My heart sank as I saw even more men lining the path all the way down to the water, where two small metal boats awaited us. Why were there so many of them?

"*This is it, Claire.*" I thought to myself, as Johnny, my mom, Major Silva and my sister's faces ran through my mind. "*You're done. This is what they've been warning you about and it's finally happening. You'll never see or talk to your family again.*"

The rain began to fall harder as they plopped me down in the bottom of the boat with a thud. I winced in pain as my thigh hit the metal sticking out of a seat. These guys were definitely not Americans, my mind reasoned. There was no way my fellow Airmen would treat me this way. I shivered again in the cold, as my lips, that were now a deep blue, shook uncontrollably under the bongie cloth that was sliding up my nose and affecting my breathing.

I knew if I had any chance at escaping, I had better do something right now. Could I fly with my hands tied behind my back and my feet bound? Why had I never thought to practice that?

Around the boat became a flurry of activity. No one said a word, but on the beach I could hear some mumbled shouting, though I couldn't quite make out what they were saying. I would have to be patient and wait for the right moment when the four guys around me were occupied. After a couple of very long minutes, my opportunity finally came. All four guys were now at the bow of the boat, talking quietly as they pulled something in. The loud plinking of the rain gave great noise coverage and I jumped at my chance.

"*Ready,*" I said to myself, as I slowly raised the top of my body off the boat floor and looked up into the dark night, the raindrops shooting like darts all around me, stinging my eyes. In one swift move I felt gravity leave my body as I stood straight up and pushed off the boat floor. "*Go Claire!*" I thought to myself, my heart jumping as I left the ground. I turned my face towards the sky that was now bathed in a brilliant lightning white.

I had managed to get a few feet in the air when I heard

one of them yell. Immediately a hand clasped around my ankle and yanked on my right leg. I looked down to see a guy hanging on for dear life. My body slowed to a stop and paused for a moment, before we both collapsed on the floor of the boat, him first and then me on top slamming my head into the bow. I instinctively curled into a ball, throbbing in pain from the egg size lump that was forming on the bottom part of my skull. All around me little stars began to sparkle and in an instant I was gone.

THE END

About the Author

Cynthia L. McDaniel is a Clarksville, Tennessee native, who resides in Northwest Indiana. When not writing, she enjoys spending time with her family, running, swimming in the Ocean, and vacations to anywhere that involves a beach. *Shooting Star* is Cynthia's third novel (part one) in her *Sky Walker* series and she looks forward to publishing part two, in the spring of 2023.

Cynthia loves to connect with her readers and other authors, and you can find her on Goodreads, on Facebook @CynthiaLMcDanielauthor, on Instagram @cynthialmcdanielauthor, or on Twitter @CynthiaLMcDani2.

Hi There!

Thank you so much for reading *Shooting Star!* I feel so honored that you would take the time to read my books and give me the opportunity to entertain you. I truly hope you are enjoying my *Sky Walker* Series. *Shooting Star* part two will be coming in the Spring of 2023, so please be watching for it!

If you wouldn't mind, I would appreciate it if you would leave a review for this book on Amazon. Reviews help Indie authors like me tremendously!

I love to connect with my readers, so please reach out to me if you have any questions or would just like to chat!

XOXO,

Cynthia

www.ingramcontent.com/pod-product-compliance
Lightning Source LLC
Chambersburg PA
CBHW022214170626
46807CB00005B/2366